THEIR EARTH

Lizzie McLaren

I AM SELF-
PUBLISHING

🐦 @iamselfpub
www.iamselfpublishing.com

My first book is dedicated to my four children,
who have contributed to my taking this leap
of faith by encouraging me, arguing with me,
and filling my home with an arkful of pets.

CONTENTS

CHAPTER 1

A TRIP

J AMES SPENT THE first morning of the summer
holidays in the hospital. He was fine. His Mum
was not. Even now she was lying on a stretcher
outside the x-ray department.

James fidgeted as he waited.

"Don't you worry now," the nurse with the long
plait had reassured him, "we'll take very good care
of her."

"It was my cat," James explained. "He's called Mr
T. My Mum tripped over him on the stairs, but he
ran off when the ambulance came."

The nurse squeezed his arm gently before
walking away.

James had not known how to say that he was actually
worrying about his cat. Mum had all the doctors

and nurses now, but Mr T had bolted straight out of the door. James imagined him hiding somewhere, afraid, not understanding what was going on.

The nurse came back and offered him some squash. Then a biscuit. Then some paper and crayons. Finally, she flicked on the TV, which James ignored. It was tuned to CBeebies and he was going to secondary school in September.

A different nurse appeared, a bald man with glasses.

"So you're James? I've got good news. Your Grandma and Grandad are on their way." He beamed at James before hurrying off.

This information confused James. He did have a Grandma and Grandad, they were his Dad's parents. He even knew they lived fairly nearby – but they never visited, because Mum did not allow it. They had fallen out around the time his Dad had disappeared. How could they even know he was at the hospital? Had his *Mum* told them?

Then it struck him. Of course, Mum had been flung downstairs! She had probably hit her head and might not be thinking properly at all. Mum could have lost her memory!

What if she had forgotten she ever fell out with his grandparents? What if she thought it was still years ago, and – a sudden chill crept along the skin of James' back and a slightly sick feeling settled into his stomach – *what if* she thought James was still just a toddler? What would happen when she saw him: all four feet of him, curly red hair, scuffed jeans and scabbed elbows? James was suddenly aware of his own body, all legs and arms, scruffy – not a cute, cuddly toddler at all. He felt his neck grow hot. He was nearly in Year 7, of course he wasn't cute, but how could he explain that to Mum – if she had lost her *memory?*

All the 'what ifs' were starting to pile up inside his brain. He had begun to breathe rather quickly, gripping the edge of the plastic seat. His legs had picked up the pace and his hands and feet had started to tingle with little, sharp pinpricks. Just then the lady nurse came back into view and swooped down on him like a hawk.

"Oh, my goodness!" To his horror she clamped something over his mouth. "Breathe into this love. It's just a paper bag, but it'll make you feel better." James gulped in several breaths, until the tingling feeling stopped, and the nurse's face became clearer. "That's it." She smiled. "I'm going to take this away now. You just had a bit of a panic attack, but there's no need to be worrying... And look who's here to see you now."

The smiling nurse stepped to the side, and what had been vague shapes behind her now emerged as two elderly people, a man and a woman. James' brain fluttered about, still recovering from his panic attack, searching for names.

"It's your Grandma and Grandad, silly!" prompted the nurse, as the old man took a step forward holding out his big right hand.

"Little Jimmy! Lord how you've grown! Good to see you lad, good to see you," he said in a gravelly voice, much too loud for a hospital.

James stared at the large, calloused hand enclosing his own. He raised his gaze upwards and scanned the grizzled face above him, taking in untidy eyebrows, a long nose and big teeth, bared in a broad grin.

"Actually," he said slowly, "my name is … *James.*"

CHAPTER 2

A DISCOVERY

M R T HAD had a dreadful morning. After having his tail painfully trodden on as he hurried downstairs, he had fled towards the kitchen in search of James and breakfast but had found neither. At that point there had begun a very loud wailing noise from the bottom of the stairs, quickly followed by James' voice yelling after the postman. Mr T registered an uneasy feeling creeping along his fur, from neck to tail, and decided that he might be better off elsewhere for a little while. He slipped rapidly over to the cat flap and shoved himself all the way through and out into the little back garden.

He immediately felt better, among the reassuring smells and sounds of Rowan Avenue. Sparrows in the branches of next door's apple tree, field mice trails across the patch of grass, woodlice rustling under the fence, and an earthworm sliding beneath some dandelions. Mr T could smell rain from last night, and the warm sun waking up. There was the faint sound of a siren in the distance which Mr T happily ignored, as he could also smell bacon cooking in one of the neighbouring houses.

Jumping up onto the fence, he was soon wobbling along on top of it, following his nose and forgetting all about his tail. Mr T plunked down onto a brick wall, to set off further afield at a fairly brisk trot, following all the scents and sounds of the waking world.

The nurse had ushered James, and his newly rediscovered grandparents, into a room where Mum had lain propped up in a very white bed with stiff sheets and solidly stuffed pillows. Much to his relief, as soon as she set eyes on him, Mum had cried out "James!" thereby proving that she did indeed remember all eleven years of him.

James was not sure whether he had expected confusion, upset, or possibly even shouting, when the adults met. But what happened instead was a short, very polite, conversation.

"Zedekiah, Emma," Mum said. "I'm sorry they just called you like that, but you were still down as next of kin at the Doctor's. Though I must say it was a relief, in the end, when we spoke."

"Helen, it's *fine*," James' grandmother said patting the quilt near Mum's hand. "This is the sort of thing you can *really* only ask of family for any length of time, and we *are* still your family, dear."

"It's quite a bad fracture apparently. They told me it might be … a few weeks," Mum said quietly.

A few weeks? James thought, looking rapidly from one adult to the other. *Weeks?* He realised the tingling feeling was still hovering at his finger ends.

"Operation tomorrow?" Grandad enquired.

"Or this evening. Then physio. I'll have to let you know – "

James realised Mum seemed unusually small, swallowed by pillows and surrounded by hospital equipment. A drip ran into her arm, and there was an alarm button by her side. Her short, dark hair not even brushed yet this morning, stuck out against the sheets, and there were grey shadows underneath her big blue eyes.

James let go of the breath he had been holding. "Mum?"

Mum squeezed his hand gently. "It's OK sweetheart. There's nothing to worry about …. I'm going to get better. Your Grandma and Grandad have – Well, I suppose, we've made up. They're very happy to have you stay with them. It's just for a little while."

James sucked in a deep breath through his nose, as he tried to make sense of the words he had just heard.

Mum's eyelids flickered, as if she were about to fall asleep, then she gave her head a little shake and continued: "They want to spend some time getting to know you… It'll be … nice."

James waited for more, but Mum's eyelids closed again. This time her breathing became deeper and he realised she had fallen asleep.

"It's the painkillers, lad," Grandad whispered loudly. "Makes her tired. We'll come back tomorrow. Give your Mum a kiss." James did as asked, before trailing out of the ward, glancing back as he went.

James soon found himself sitting in the back of a taxi beside his Grandma, who was alternately dozing and apologising for 'nodding off'. Grandad sat in the front passenger seat, deep in conversation with the driver about rush hour traffic. Gazing out of the window, James saw that they were driving past Rowan Avenue and instantly remembered Mr T.

"Grandma!"

James startled Grandma into sitting bolt upright.

"What is it Jimmy?" She peered at him over the top of her spectacles. Her eyes, which were creased at the corners like paper, bored into him teacher-like. James turned away to watch the junction as they sped past it.

"It's, er, it's my cat. He's still there - I mean, at home!"

Grandma relaxed into her seat and smiled at him. James watched the little puckers of skin around her mouth all stretch out smoothly when she did so.

"Oh. Is that all? We'll have to go home later anyway. You'll need some clothes - perhaps some toys? We can find Mr T then for you." Grandma patted his leg before settling back to rest her eyes once more. As James contemplated his sleeping Grandma, however, his own forehead wrinkled into a frown.

How did Grandma know what his cat was called ...? James turned away and watched the receding streets.

That evening, at his grandparents' home, James unpacked. He had expected to find himself in a sort of dark and musty old-people's house, with lots of ornaments and flowery things on the sofas – but it wasn't like that at all. Everywhere was spotlessly clean, the kitchen organised with military precision. Even the dishcloth had a hook. There were no frills or knick-knacks, but a very comfy sofa and chairs in the living room, and the bedroom he was given was larger than his own at home. It had a double bed and an armchair, as well as two chests of drawers and a wardrobe. The carpet was thick and his bed soft and springy.

James put away the few things he had brought, and surveyed the clean, cosy room. Immediately, he thought of his single bed, his jumbled wardrobe and, of course, Mum. And it was just like a big hole slowly opened up where his stomach should have been. He hugged his arms tight around himself, as if he could stop the hole getting any larger.

James couldn't ever remember not having said 'goodnight' to Mum or giving her a hug before heading off to bed. He didn't feel like an-almost-at-secondary-school boy at all now. He felt much more like the little boy he had been remembering earlier that day.

At the bottom of his bag James found a slightly threadbare dinosaur plushy, called Dino, that he'd had for ever. He must have stuffed it in there as he grabbed things from home. He was suddenly very grateful to have Dino and curled up in the armchair with him, allowing his mind to wander back to Mr T. Where would Mr T be right now? At home, James hoped very much, eating his cat food at last.

Em, James' Grandma, came up and found James fast asleep in the chair. With Zed's help, she got their young grandson into bed, then sat on the edge of the quilt while he drifted back off to sleep.

"Grandma," muttered James, barely awake enough to talk. "Did you … find … Mr T … mm?" But he drifted off again, and was soon deeply asleep, not even dreaming of his cat.

Em took a moment to smooth down the sides of the quilt. Zed squeezed her shoulder, saying: "Come on, old girl, we need to check on a few things. He'll be fine, till morning, and we've work to do."

Later that night, James woke up. He reached for the water bottle he always kept on his bedside table, patted around with his hand in the dark for a bit, then tried to work out what was wrong. After a moment, as his eyes became used to the gloom, he remembered where he was.

He supposed he would have to go down to the kitchen to get himself a glass of water, so popped his feet out of bed and padded across to the door, which was just a tiny bit ajar and letting in a glow from downstairs. Which was odd, surely? Because it was very late.

James clicked on his bedroom light and squinted at the little clock on the chest of drawers. It was nearly 1.00 a.m. Across the landing, he could see the door to his grandparents' room was half open, and their bed was still neatly made.

He tip-toed downstairs.

The TV was off. The glow was coming from a single table lamp in the living room. The house was very quiet.

He crossed to the kitchen, opened the door, and switched on the light. No-one. Taking a glass from the cupboard, he filled it, and started sipping his water.

After a few mouthfuls, he set it down on the draining board and turned around to see through the kitchen doorway, to the living room, and to the hallway beyond.

Where *could* they be?

James knew his grandparents were not used to having him here. Had they forgotten about him and decided to take a walk, late, in the dark? But why would anyone do that? Or, had they just … gone out - to a pub, or somewhere? He knew Mum never did any of these things but, well, she was his Mum. If they had gone out, presumably they must come back soon though?

James suddenly felt it would be very awkward if they did come back and he was standing around in the kitchen, like a … like a grown up, waiting for teenagers to come home. So, not knowing what else to do, he went back to bed.

Later still, James woke up again, to go to the bathroom. He became immediately aware of snoring from the room across the landing. The third time he climbed into bed that night, he had a smile on his face, as he was lulled into a deep sleep by Grandad's regular growling.

The following day, James decided to ask Grandad what he and Grandma did after James had gone to bed. He blinked several times at Grandad's reply.

"Oh, nothing exciting. We were in bed soon after you, young man. Just time for a cup of tea and a browse through the paper."

James didn't know what to say, so said nothing.

The next day they visited Rowan Avenue again, but Mr T had not yet returned. James pressed his lips together and felt a sort of lump form in his chest.

"The cat food's gone!" called Grandad from the kitchen. "We probably just missed him, Jimmy lad ... Not to worry!"

James let out a deep sigh as they locked the door.

Two days ...

CHAPTER 3

MR T HAS A BAD DAY

M R T was not as agile as some cats. Nor was he as young as he once was, and nowadays walked with a slight waddle, due to living a life divided mostly between dozing and eating. He still thought of himself, however, as the sprightly young cat of his early years and imagined he was stealthily stalking his prey through the endless back gardens. By late morning he was some two and a half miles from Rowan Avenue and plonked himself down on someone's brick wall to groom his fur. Having failed to find the source of the bacon smell, he had stumbled across the remains of a ham sandwich poking out of a fallen dustbin. So things could be worse.

Mr T knew of cats who walked for four or five miles every evening, but he was about at the limit of his own usual wanderings. He was just thinking that perhaps it was time to about turn and head for home, when he spied a familiar form waiting at the corner of the wall ahead of him, facing his way.

Mr T strolled on a little further to sit down in front of the man in the leather jacket, who raised one of his large, gnarly hands in greeting. The man, who had been watching Mr T wandering along for a while, leaned on the wall and sighed.

"What have you done *now?*"

Mr T sat up very straight and raised his chin to look levelly at the man who addressed him.

"Hrrrm. Other than maintain deep cover and report back to you, regularly, for half a lifetime?" Mr T's voice purred like a distant car's engine.

His companion rubbed a hand through thick, grey-and-black, peppery hair, as he regarded Mr T.

"Well *Agent*, there's deep cover … and then there's, what's known in the trade as 'going native.' Generally, an agent on surveillance does his best *not* to take out his protectee's Mother." The man, who Mr T knew as Agent Zed, was old with bushy eyebrows – from beneath which his deep blue eyes stared, unblinking at Mr T. Mr T shuffled about on the wall, conscious that his discomfort had little to do with being seated on bricks. "Well," the old guy broke the silence, "we can discuss it in the debrief. You're being recalled. Your protectee is not returning home for some time."

As he said this, he bent down and scooped up Mr T, who drooped like a damp rag, as he was deposited on a blanket inside a large black container, on the back of a huge black motorbike. Mr T felt the carrier bounce as Agent Zed positioned himself on the machine's seat before it roared off down the road. He pawed thoughtfully at the familiar tartan wool before settling down, with a sigh, for the ride.

Mr T was delivered to The Operations Room where he was interviewed by Agent Em, who spent some time getting to the bottom of how the morning's incident had occurred.

Mr T could see no way to avoid telling the truth: that he had run downstairs and barged through Helen's legs, with no regard whatsoever for Health and Safety, because – well – because he had been in a hurry to get to his *breakfast.* At this point, Agent Em had thrown her arms in the air, in a dramatic gesture that Mr T thought was probably a bad sign.

It seemed that Helen was now in hospital, as a result of the encounter, and that James had therefore become their house guest. Agent Em glared at Mr T, from behind her glasses which only magnified the expression.

I really am not, mused Mr T, *having my best day ever.*

"Confined to quarters!" said Agent Em at last. "You'll stay here and make yourself useful. Then, assuming you are up to the task, we will discuss - *discuss* mind you - the *possibility* of your returning to duty. Is that clear?"

"As crystal," muttered Mr T behind his whiskers. His pale, gold irises tracked Agent Em's progress as she left the room and, when he was absolutely sure she had closed the door, he added:

"But I think you underestimate my boy. Hrrrm?"

A little while after the debrief Zed was standing at the kitchen sink, looking out over the tidy lawn and neatly trimmed privet hedge, when the noise of a couple of sparrows arguing in an apple tree was suddenly overtaken by a noticeably higher note – it made a rapid 'scree-scree-scree' sound.

"Em!" Zed called out, but in a low, gruff voice. Em stuck her head around the door to the kitchen.

"Where's the lad?" he continued.

"He's watching TV dear. I just gave him a yoghurt."

"Good. I'll keep an eye on him. It's an alert. You go."

Em nodded and slipped the rest of herself through the doorway.

Pulling on a pair of scuffed trainers from the utility room, and grabbing a back-pack that hung over the shoe rack, she exited through the back door.

The call came again, louder outside.

Em pinpointed a small grey shape high up in the sky. She made a ring out of her thumb and middle finger, placed them in her mouth against her tongue, and blew a series of short piercing whistles. The small grey shape swept down to hover over Em's head, revealing itself as a kestrel.

"I'm coming, Cass," Em sang out and the bird shot off for maybe half a mile, hovered, then returned. "OK Cass, I have it now," she said, raising her arm in salute. Em set off at a swift jog that would have stunned most passers-by had they known her age. The kestrel, Cass, had perched on top of a lamp-post. Beneath it, in the gutter, there was something dark that might have been a discarded hoodie.

It was not.

Em went closer, kneeled down, and removed a blanket from inside her back-pack. Wrapping the small form with care, she transferred it into the roomy interior of the bag, waving once more to the tiny brown, grey and white bird, then headed swiftly for home. Cass opened his wings and lifted off, high into the pale blue sky.

That evening, James only pretended to settle down to sleep. Instead, after his grandparents went downstairs, he tiptoed across the landing and peered through the banisters. He saw his grandparents disappear into the kitchen but soon return carrying mugs. Both sipped their tea, reading.

James was about to give up when Grandad put down his book.

"OK then, Em?" Grandad said.

Grandma nodded and Grandad went over to the tall bookshelf against the long wall of the living room, and gave it a shove! It moved smoothly sideways, revealing a door. Grandma took a key from her pocket, unlocked it, and they both went inside. Then the door closed, and the bookcase moved itself back into place.

James sat completely still for a moment, then trudged very slowly back to his room and sat, unsure of what to do, on the edge of his bed. His comic lay open on the floor. *Iron Man* stared back at him, blasting his way into his arch enemy's lair.

If I were Iron Man, thought James, *I wouldn't stay hiding here in my room, would I?*

He stood up again and headed for the stairs. In the living room he stopped beside the bookcase, took a sharp breath, and shoved. The large piece of furniture slid rapidly and easily along the wall, then shuddered to a stop, with a clunk. Not a single book fell off. James breathed out, listening. There was no sound from the other side.

The door he had revealed was just like the other two doors in the room, but with a keyhole. James held his fist up to knock, then changed his mind and simply opened the door, wide.

Whatever he had expected, it was *not* this!

The room was lit by a ghoulish red glow, in the middle of which a circle of bright, white light revealed two masked figures bent over a table with something lying on it. As his vision refocused, James realised the object of their attention was distinctly … *furry*.

Sweeping his eyes over the rest of the room he next registered a very familiar shape on the far side.

It appeared red right now but, in daylight, James knew for certain it would be a light ginger.

"Mr T?" he gasped.

The two masked figures swung around. As they did, the bright light exposed a glistening steel scalpel in the hand of the nearest one. James forgot all about being *Iron Man,* and reached out a steadying hand to grasp at the door.

The figure with the knife pulled down its mask, the thick lenses of a pair of glasses reflecting the blood-red light, and spoke:

"Oh … dearie me! This *is* a pickle!"

CHAPTER 4

MASKS AND A SCALPEL

Everyone in the room was paused, caught out, frozen under the ghoulish light. Each appeared to be waiting for the others to break the spell. Mr T's ears twitched, as if the room were full of static. In no particular hurry, he lifted his head up off his cushion, and addressed Zed in a low purr.

"Cat's out of the bag now, hrrrm, I'd say?"

"*Mr T!*"

This last was from James, his face a picture of confusion, as he spotted Mr T – who stood up, stretched, then glanced happily around the room in general.

Agent Em glanced from James, to Mr T, and back again, saying: "Oh … dearie me! This *is* a pickle!"

"Grandma …?"

Mr T sat down on his haunches to better watch the entertainment. *Hrrrm. Let's see you explain this*, he thought contentedly.

The taller figure took a step forward, pulling down its mask too, and revealing James' Grandad's grizzled face.

 "Jimmy, er … aren't you, supposed to be in bed, young man?"

James stared at Grandad and said nothing. Grandad carried on.

"Ah … well, now you're here … you're, erm - you're doubtless wondering, what's going on, eh?"

James continued to watch Grandad. Grandad tried a hearty smile. Then a half-hearted chuckle. James remained silent.

"Right. Ah … Right. Yes. Well, er - as you can see - We've *found* Mr T! That's good news, isn't it?"

James glanced towards his pet. Yes, that was good news. News that James felt he should probably have been told. He moved his gaze back to Grandad.

"So, anyway, you can say a proper hello, in the morning. But, um, well. I really think it's time you went to sleep, now ... It's very late -"

James raised a single eyebrow, which stayed there, and Grandma cleared her throat before taking a step forward to join them.

"Zed dear, I think it's a bit *too late* for that. We've been rumbled." She smiled at James. "We're sorry we couldn't tell you dear. But, you see, it's secret ... From everyone. Still, now you're here - Do you want help? I do need to get back to this little one before the anaesthetic wears off ..."

James took a few steps forward and peered around his grandparents. There was a small, black cat, flat out and fast asleep, on what was clearly an operating table.

"Are you - a vet?" gasped James, though for the life of him he couldn't work out why anyone needed a secret vet.

"Yes!" boomed Grandad, "That's exactly what she is, yes! A vet ... Your Grandma is ... a secret vet."

Grandma shot a sideways glance at Grandad.

"A *specialist* vet," she added. "I'm performing some new and experimental procedures … to help animals who have been injured." She beckoned James closer. "They're not widely known, and they're certainly not on the market for normal vets to use. But they're quite safe. We're, er, testing them out - to make sure they work properly. Do you follow?"

James nodded, still gazing at the sleeping cat. It was black with a white patch on its chest that moved slowly up and down as it breathed. The side of its face he could see was torn, as if from a fight or an accident. James felt a little catch in his throat, and swallowed. The blood had been cleaned away to reveal small shards of white bone poking through the skin of the cheekbone. There was a raw, red gash gleaming through the black fur above its shoulder.

"What should I do, Grandma?" he asked.

"Good boy!" Grandma grinned at James. "You can start by scrubbing up. Grandad will show you."

James' Grandad took him over to a sink in the corner, also finding him a mask and a rather large, green apron.

"Sorry we didn't wake you when we found Mr T." Grandad apologised. "We thought maybe Grandma should … check him over first but, er, don't worry, he's fine."

"Oh," said James. "OK."

Behind James, Agent Zed swept the back of his hand across his forehead and made an exaggerated "thumbs-up" gesture to the room at large.

"Hrrrm," said Mr T, narrowing his eyes at Zed. "Good catch ... But you do seem to have missed the *teensy* fact that James is *inside* the operations room now? The only way you could make things worse would be by - oh, I don't know - letting him *join in?* Though I have to say, it's *perfectly fine* by me!"

Agent Zed ignored Mr T and ushered James towards the operating table. Mr T settled down on his cushion and felt the warm, cosy sense of having lapped up a puddle of cream. Which was odd, as all he had eaten was chicken.

"Now, Jimmy," said Agent Em, "I hope you're not squeamish?"

She aimed her scalpel towards the sleeping cat's face.

CHAPTER 5

JAMES LEARNS
A SECRET

J AMES' FEET WERE trapped beneath a boulder. He was trying to wiggle one foot loose, when his eyelids snapped open, and he realised that his ankles were in fact caught under a large, snoring, ginger cat. With a rush, he remembered all about the previous night. James shoved Mr T sideways, and jumped up, scrabbling for clean clothes in the drawer.

Despite the late night previously, his grandparents were clearly already awake to continue their work.

When James arrived downstairs, the study door was uncovered and *ajar*. The 'operations room,' as James now knew it, was there for him to enter freely. So he did. Grandma and Grandad were busy inside. The infrared lights were off and a very efficient fluorescent bulb lit up every corner, including the cage containing a sleeping black cat with a white patch on her chest. James poked his fingers through the bars and stroked her fur.

"Morning young Jim," Grandad greeted James. He gestured towards the sleeping cat. "She's doing really well. Your Grandma's a star."

Grandma made a no-nonsense sort of noise and bustled over to James to enquire whether or not he'd had breakfast.

"Well, you'll eat first, then. You had a good old sleep you know, it's nearly ten. Then," Grandma tugged her pullover sleeves down level with her wrists. "We'll have a little chat. Don't look so worried! We'll be seeing your Mum today …. So - we need to get all our ducks in a row!"

James had no idea where ducks came into anything, but was far too happy to care, so went to find food and gulp it down. When he came back though, the study door was closed. Grandma and Grandad were sitting on the sofa, gesturing for him to join them.

"So," began Grandad, "Grandma and I were wondering. How much did you … take in? Of what we were doing, last night?" He waited, plucking carelessly at the sofa cover.

"Well," James began, "I know … Grandma is, a vet, now." He screwed his mouth sideways, thinking. "I don't know why you can't tell Mum though? I mean – *she* was a vet nurse … Oh, except that it's secret, of course." He paused, and chewed on his cheek. "And, you said you were doing, like … research. So - when you make the animals better, you use stuff Mum's vet place can't?" James wrinkled his nose. "That's it really … Oh - and *you found Mr T!* Where was he, anyway?"

While James was speaking, Mr T himself had entered the room and was currently curled up on one of the armchairs.

"Good lad," said Grandma. "You're exactly right! As far as it goes, anyway. You know about the operations now … But there's something else we, we ought to tell you, before we see your Mum? So we can, sort out a few things –" Grandma's voice trailed off and she looked across at Grandad, who took over.

"Jimmy ... Your Mum *does* know about Grandma, and her animals. She always did. No - wait a minute – " James had opened his mouth. "Now, it shouldn't be us telling you this. If anyone was going to, it should be your Mum. But it hasn't worked out that way. So … I just want you to remember. We only all kept a secret from you to *take care of* you." Grandad took a breath and shifted in his seat to get comfortable. James stayed quiet. He had not the slightest idea what he might be about to hear next. "Your Dad," Grandad began again, and James stared even harder, "used to work for Lifelink – that's, with the animals – too. Er, as well as, his work with computers, you see. But his work was more … out in the field. He couldn't say anything, he wasn't allowed."

"Just like we shouldn't be saying anything now, not really," Grandma cut in. James noticed her hands were clasped tightly together. "Jimmy, you do understand? Grandad and I are taking a risk here? We are trusting you. It is *very* important you keep whatever we tell you to yourself. Well, and us, obviously. And your Mum of course … But – can you do that?"

James nodded. Grandma sat back to let Grandad continue.

"So, anyway - your Dad was, a secret agent – "

"Sorry what?" James' mouth hung open while his brain found some more words. "What? With … ? With *animals?*"

"Well, yes," Grandad confirmed. "But only certain animals - only the ones that had been through the operations room. We - we monitor them." Grandad opened both his hands out, palms up, as if that might help him explain. "Some of the implants help us, to do that."

"Like microchips!" James said quickly, hearing something he could grasp.

"Yes," said Grandma. "Microchips. And – a few other bits and pieces. Like the eye-cameras for instance."

James blinked. "Cameras?"

"Mm, if an animal has an injured eye, and if we can't save it. What we *can* do is replace it, with – well, a sort-of-robot eyeball. It will work just like a real one. The animal will be able to see again."

"But you said *camera*," pursued James.

"Yes I did." Grandma nodded. "That's where the software engineering part came in. Some prosthetic eyes can also transmit what they are seeing. So, we can receive pictures. Here at Ops - the operations room. It's not just about surgery, you see, Ops. It's the … the hub. The place we run things from." Grandma looked back at Grandad, who took up the story yet again.

James pulled his legs up onto the sofa and leaned his chin on his hands, staring hard, from one grandparent to the other.

"So your Dad would monitor the screens. And he could see where the animals were and, sometimes, what they saw ... And, occasionally, that meant your Dad would, would know about things, going on. That shouldn't be," said Grandad.

"What? Like ... *burglaries?*" James interrupted.

"Possibly," said Grandad. "Possibly burglary. And whenever he saw anything that - needed attention, he'd go and, er, attend to it." Grandad fell silent for a moment, as if thinking. James was thinking too, making sense of all the new information.

"So ... my Dad, was like a – policeman? Like CID, or, something ... ? Grandad? What *did* actually happen, to my Dad?" James had been thinking how exciting and mysterious all this made his Dad, until he realised that dealing with burglars and criminals was not at all safe and could explain quite a lot. "Mum said he went to work and he never came home. That no-one could find him. That the police gave up!" His Dad's disappearance was sounding much more understandable now.

"I honestly don't know lad." Grandad sighed, his face seemed empty, tired somehow. "You know as much as we do about that ... The police, they couldn't find him. And neither could we ... But your Grandma and I, we've never given up hope that we'll see him again. I know your Mum hasn't either - and neither should you."

Grandma spoke, reaching out to touch Grandad's arm as she did so.

"That's what all this is about, my dear. Your Mum didn't want you to get involved ... In case, well, in case you disappeared one day, like your Dad did. She thought, if you knew, about his work – and if you thought it was exciting – well, you might want to do the same job. She was frightened that something might happen to you. Do you see?"

"Ye-es," replied James. "I do ... I don't want Mum to lose me either. But, Grandma. I'm way too young to do that job! Aren't I?"

Grandma burst out laughing, and James felt like a breeze had swept through the room brightening it up.

"Well … yes dear. You are *now*. But one day you won't be,"

Grandad was still studying him. "You got any questions, lad?"

James had.

"When we see Mum, can't we just tell her? That I'm way too young to be a secret agent … so she shouldn't worry? And - if it's OK - can I keep helping Grandma with the animals? Just for the summer holidays? Please?"

Grandma and Grandad promised they would at least ask. Grandma chuckled.

"I, for one, would love having a little helper, Jimmy. It will be like the old days, when my Jake assisted. He used to take care of the animals in recovery too."

Mr T, who had been quiet this whole time, addressed Agent Em and spoke in a firm voice.

"You do know? It won't stop at that. Don't you, hrrrm? I can feel it in my fur … He's a speaker alright." He padded over and rubbed his nose against James' ankles.

The boy himself was following Agent Zed towards the Ops door, quite unaware of Mr T's announce-ment.

Agent Em pursed her lips but did not respond.

CHAPTER 6

EVIE HEARS VOICES

Evie McAdam was what Agent Em would have called "a tough nut to crack". Quiet and moody by nature, at sixteen Evie was more than ready to become an adult. All she wanted was a job and a normal life of her own choosing, mostly because Evie felt she had had nothing normal in life as far back as she could remember. 'As far back' would be to the children's home she ended up in, when she was left outside a police station in the middle of the night. A baby wrapped in a sofa throw and tucked into a box. There was no note. She didn't even have a name. The Matron at the children's home registered her as Eve, because she was found on December 24th. McAdam was chosen in honour of the founder of the children's home. Had Morag McAdam been alive to actually meet Evie later on, she might have sighed slightly at the choice.

As a child in a children's home, however lovely the staff are (and the staff of Oak Manor *were* lovely) and, however well they cared for the children, nothing could change the fact that each child had already been abandoned - whether by choice, or accident. Each child there began life at a distinct disadvantage in the world. By the time she could talk, however, Evie understood that she was even more disadvantaged than the children around her. Those children had come to Oak Manor with names. Some with toys, or clothes. Some even with letters or mementos they could hold onto for ever. Evie had none of these things, and the cruellest of children on the worst of days would remind her, despite risking the wrath of Matron.

So it was that even the nursery helpers, those especially kind ladies who cared for the little ones, whispered that Evie "had been born in a bad mood and it had stuck." It came as no surprise, to any of the staff at Oak Manor over the years, that Evie was neither fostered nor adopted.

By the time she was twelve, Evie was the tallest girl in the home, awkward and gangly. She often sat crouched in a corner, spiderlike with her limbs tucked up, watching the others but not joining in. The other children learned to ignore her when she refused to join in with their games. Matron had worried so much about Evie that she had had the doctor conduct tests, to see if Evie had a medical condition that could explain her behaviour and be treated. The doctor, however, reported that Evie was mentally and physically in fine health, a 'typical moody teenager.'

After that, the staff had made the best of it and decided to look only at the positives. Evie did well in school, she was fairly tidy, she even helped the little kids sometimes (if they fell over for instance, or if someone picked on them). Really, she was quite a *nice* girl. She just rarely smiled. And wouldn't know what a conversation was if she fell into the middle of one.

Evie, they agreed, was just a bit … odd.

Evie herself knew that she was rather more than odd. She was much more, well, an out-and-out weirdo: which was something she had discovered around the age of thirteen. It wasn't enough that she should suddenly have a growth spurt and end up a good head taller than anyone else her age. No. *She* had to start hearing voices as well.

Only a few months after the doctor had done his tests to determine Evie was, without question, utterly normal – Evie herself could have told him, beyond a shadow of doubt, that she was anything but.

It started one day in the garden. As usual, Evie was sitting on her own. She was wondering whether to slope off indoors and read in her room, or stay where she was perched up in the old cherry tree. She was watching the little kids on the grass below, filling plastic cups with daisies and feeding them to their toys, when she became aware of the argument. Up until then, all she had heard was the background hum of traffic from the main road, the chattering kids on the lawn, and the chirping of small birds as they fluttered between the two old trees in the garden. Yet, very gradually, she became aware that there were also two separate, distinctly high-pitched voices in amongst the noise. Evie could clearly hear their words.

"You leave it alone, it's mine." Then, "I saw it first. You snatched it. It's not fair, it's mine. I saw it first." The argument became both voices simply repeating the word 'mine' several times, before fading out, as if the owners had just wandered off. Evie scanned the garden. She expected to see the tops of two small heads somewhere nearby, fighting over a tennis ball, or a stick, or some other valuable object. But the only children were the tea-party kids, who were still giggling happily together.

Weird, thought Evie, and didn't dwell on it.

Just a day or so later, though, Evie started to think maybe she *should* take notice after all.

A couple of prospective foster parents had come to collect one of the boys and, as was usual, they were spending a little time with Matron in the garden room, a room with big windows that opened onto the lawn. The couple had a Labrador and they had been allowed to bring him in. Some of the younger children had gathered round to pet him. They were very excited, but had been told to keep their voices down. So they were whispering and laughing, as they scratched behind the dog's ears and stroked his rather broad, golden back.

Evie was half-watching them, when she thought she picked out a new voice amongst the others. She only noticed because this voice was much deeper, so could not possibly have been one of the children.

"Thank goodness we're not taking you *all* home. I'm prepared to give one of you a try, but I need my peace and quiet these days ... Don't you know dogs generally like a scratch behind the ears? Yes – like that. Maybe it's not *such* a bad idea ..." The deep voice went rumbling on beneath the chatter.

For a few seconds Evie assumed she had heard the foster-Dad and was shocked, and a little bit delighted, by his rudeness. Then she realised only the Mum was talking. The Dad was drinking his tea. So *who* was speaking? She suddenly realised that – whoever it was – they were doing a *voice-over* for the dog. It was also pretty funny, exactly the sort of thing a dog might say.

Evie jumped up off the bench she had been sitting on and walked all the way around the garden, peering behind bushes and anywhere she could think of, to find the culprit. By the time she'd checked the whole garden, though, the couple had gone and the voice long stopped. Evie had a mystery!

It happened again a couple of times. Once was at night, when everyone was *supposed* to be asleep. It was warm, and her bedroom window was open a little, when Evie heard voices from below. By the time she had scrambled out of bed and crammed her face against the glass, to peer downwards, she could see no-one. Just a stray cat vanishing over the wall.

No-one in the street. No-one awake in the house.

That, Evie decided, *was* eerie. She was quite glad when she heard no more voices for several weeks. They came back, though, every now and again. Evie gradually realised that they were always voice-overs for various animals.

Eventually, by the time she was hearing them most days, she also realised that there was never anyone else around. There simply could not be one person, always with her, never seen, who voiced all the creatures she encountered during her everyday life.

So, then Evie knew that the voices existed only inside her head.

The discovery was in fact not as terrifying as it might have been because, by then, Evie had become quite used to hearing them. They made entertaining moments in her otherwise unexciting day. So she decided to say nothing, and to let them stay. If she spoke up, Matron would doubtless haul her back to the doctor. He would give her medication to take the voices away – of that she was certain. Evie kept quiet, and the voices kept talking – right up until she was sixteen and allowed to leave Oak Manor, for good.

The day Evie moved out was very sad for all the Oak Manor staff. Moody and sullen she might have been, but she had been theirs from the beginning of her life, and it felt like losing a member of the family. Matron had found Evie a studio flat, on subsidised rent, plus an apprenticeship in the local Spar shop. Before leaving, Evie stiffly hugged various members of staff, then Matron herself drove to the flat and helped unpack the bags.

"I got you these, Evie," Matron said, handing her a pair of brand-new trainers and a sturdy waterproof back-pack. Evie took them from her and held them close. Normally a very no-nonsense sort of lady, Matron hesitated by the door to the flat, saying finally: "You're to come to supper. Any night you fancy." She turned to go, but changed her mind, adding, "And you're to call me, if you need - anything, at all. You hear?" Evie nodded and Matron took a step onto the pavement. "I know it's what you want, but it's very young to be living on your own, Evie. The lady at the Spar was lovely though. She's certain you'll be a big help and I told her you're a good learner. You're to see her Monday morning, at seven o'clock … You won't forget now?" Matron had already told Evie this at least twice before.

"I won't forget," Evie said, squeezing her lips into the shrug that generally passed for a grin. "And, er, thank you. You know, for… everything." Evie held the door open.

Matron left, turning around to raise her hand twice on the short walk to the kerb. She climbed into the driver's seat and leaned across to wave, as Evie made a thumbs-up sign and closed the door.

Evie woke up, on the first morning in her new home, to blue skies and sunshine. She dressed, then went over to the front door to view the world that she was about to call her own.

Sitting on the doorstep was a tortoiseshell cat. Evie flicked a hand above its head and said a half-hearted 'Shoo!' The cat remained where it was. It didn't even look up. It then stepped inside the flat and headed towards the kitchen.

Oh, what? thought Evie, *It must belong to the previous tenant. What do I do now?*

She rifled through the kitchen cupboard and opened a tin of tuna, spooning it onto a saucer, and placing it on the floor. The cat shot over and began eating, like it hadn't had food for some time. Evie took another saucer and filled it with water, then sat on one of the chairs and watched the cat while it licked round the edges for the last traces of fish.

"Well," said Evie, "what should I call you, then?"

"Artemis," said the tortoiseshell in a clear, rather nasal voice, staring straight into Evie's deep brown, startled eyes. "But I can't stay long."

This was a whole new level of crazy.

CHAPTER 7

NO TURNING BACK

Em, Zed and James were perched nervously on three red plastic chairs lined up beside Helen's hospital bed. They had just finished explaining everything that had happened, and how James now knew about Ops and his grandparents' secret. Helen had listened to the last half of it with her eyes shut but was clearly awake, by the way her lips had sometimes closed into a tight line, and her forehead had wrinkled as she listened. Even the nurses had left them alone, sensing that important family matters were being discussed.

Finally, Helen sat up and looked at them - after all three had fallen silent - scanning their faces one after another.

For just a moment, if he had not known better, James would have said Mum was about to laugh. But that made no sense. And, indeed, instead she took a deep breath and spoke to them in a steady, very serious voice.

"I see from your faces that at least you understand the gravity of the situation. I should have known better myself, than to expect you to be able to keep Lifelink a secret from your grandson for six weeks. Though it's no use crying over spilled milk I suppose." She sighed deeply, glanced at James for a moment, then turned back to his grandparents and raised her head and shoulders to sit more upright. "Emma, Zedekiah - just you keep my boy *safe*. Alright? That's all I ask. And James – yes, you may help your Grandmother. But you only ever, *ever* do as your Grandma tells you." She slumped back onto the pillows and said under her breath, to no-one really: "Oh, if I could just *walk!*"

James wasn't sure what Mum meant she would do if she could walk? Take him home, presumably, so he wasn't staying at Grandma's. While he was - of course - very sorry for Mum, he had to admit things hadn't turned out too badly as far as he was concerned. James turned his attention back to the adults' conversation. Grandma was telling Mum that James would do nothing dangerous during operations.

"It isn't as if we rescue animals that often, anyway - and there's nothing else he can get involved in."

This last comment only made James wonder what 'else' there could be? But he was wise enough to know when he was ahead.

Mr T was delighted to see James bouncing around in a very good mood when he returned to Cromwell Street. The injured stray was up and around too now and James spent time stroking her and talking to her, while Mr T watched from a cushion.

"It's OK Mr T," chattered James, "You're still my number one cat! I'm just spending time with this little girl until she gets better."

"I should think so too," muttered Mr T, despite knowing he was talking to himself. The black and white queen purred as James tickled her chin, but she said nothing.

Inside Evie's flat, Artemis talked some more.

Evie listened while the cat calmly explained that the voices "in her head" were, in fact, coming from the animals themselves.

Evie then explained to Artemis that this information would mean a lot more if it weren't for the possibility that it was, in fact, coming from one of those voices inside her head.

The cat sighed.

"I see." it said. "Ask me to do something. Jump onto a chair .... Walk round the table ... Something like that."

"OK," said Evie. "Why?"

"Because, if I do it, then you'll know I can understand you."

"Stand on your head," said Evie.

"*What?* Oh for kittens' sake! It has to be something I can physically *do!*" Artemis flexed her front claws, in, out.

"Lie down ... Stand up ... Sit down … Stand up ... Hah!" said Evie, as Artemis followed instructions. "So … So, how do I know I'm not *hallucinating* now instead?"

"Because. I *didn't.* Stand on my *head.*"

"Hah!" Evie cried, "You're right! Best day *ever!*" Evie jumped up to sit on the counter then hopped down again grinning widely "So. What now?"

"Well, I'm off. Done my bit. Told you you're not bonkers." Artemis arched her back briefly then headed for the door. She looked at it, pointedly.

Evie didn't move.

"You're just … going? You spoke to me. And now, you're leaving?"

"Yes -" Artemis said. "Oh, sorry. Thank you, for the breakfast. Long walk. Much appreciated. Er - door?"

Evie moved towards the door and slowly gripped the handle.

"But ... But I have questions," she said. "Who can I ask - questions?"

There was long second or two of silence.

"Just about anybody. Let's see … so far you've understood birds, cats, dogs, humans … ? Usually if you can hear them, they can hear you. So - ?" Evie noticed Artemis' tail twitch, once. She edged forward and cracked the door open enabling Artemis to slip out into the sunshine.

Evie watched the small grey form disappear along the pavement, then plodded back to the kitchen. Her hands opened cupboards and found a bowl, some cereal, milk from the fridge. She had been sitting at the table for some minutes, with a spoon raised half way to her lips, before she let it clatter back into the bowl, splattering the table with milk. She stood up abruptly.

"*I can talk with animals!*"

Evie grabbed her new trainers, dragging them onto her feet, desperate to get out into the sunshine and find someone, anyone, to talk to ... as long as they had fur, or maybe feathers. Or - a shell, possibly?

In the local park, however, Evie soon discovered it was not easy to test out her ability after all. Small birds were hopeless. She tried to interrupt a few, but they ignored her. They seemed to squabble a lot. Over twigs, other birds, branches, worms, insects ... but no real conversations. Evie decided she needed something more cat-like, but the only real option in the park was a dog. The trouble with dogs was that they came with owners and Evie needed to approach a dog alone. So she decided to lurk in the bushes and wait and see.

The first dog to come wandering through sniffed at her jeans disinterestedly but did not appear to hear her at all. Next, the greenery crashed about as a large Pointer bounded in after a tennis ball, coming to a juddering halt just in front of her. Evie whispered to it.

"Sorry, er, have you - got a minute?"

The dog muttered around the ball that was now in its mouth. "Do I *look* like I have a minute?" He was gone before Evie could think of a response.

Shortly after that, Evie spied a community policeman wandering the perimeter of the park. She had to choose between crouching down and trying to remain completely hidden, to avoid awkward questions, or strolling out from the undergrowth. Grabbing a piece of the undergowth as she went, Evie pushed her way noisily through the greenery just before the policeman arrived. He stopped, blank-faced, as she burst from the bushes waving a handful of weeds at him.

"Oh, hello!" she spluttered, "Er … *floribundum park, er, Parker … variety* …. School project!" Evie headed swiftly towards the exit, leaving the policeman gazing after her, before he began peering closely at the shrubbery.

Clearly, this was going to be trickier than she had at first thought.

Evie went back to the flat for a coffee and a think. She very much wished she knew anyone with a pet.

The following morning, Evie dutifully arose at six o'clock to ensure that she was freshly showered, breakfasted and neatly dressed in time to arrive at the Spar by five minutes to seven. She felt rather fluttery inside. This was the start of her independence, her first paid employment. Her fingers drummed repeatedly on her thigh as she waited for the store to open its doors.

At seven o'clock precisely, the door was opened by a middle-aged lady with blonde highlights, rather a lot of make-up and a broad smile across her round face.

"Ah, Evie!" said the lady cheerfully. "In you come. I have been so looking forward to meeting you at last."

The lady, who introduced herself as Kath, was warm and loud so Evie did her best to be the same. This resulted in quite an acceptable smile, a quiet 'Hello' and a 'Thank you' as she followed Kath inside. There was a man, maybe a bit older than Evie, hanging up packets of batteries behind the till.

"That's Ayaan, he's holding the fort this morning, so you and I can have a chat in the back room." Ayaan smiled at Evie who gave a small nod as she followed Kath through the plastic swing doors and into a little room with a sink, a kettle and a couple of easy chairs.

"So," Kath began, "have a seat and I'll pop the kettle on. First things first though, I assume you've met Artemis?"

"Um," said Evie, as she dropped into the nearest chair, "I … sorry? Er - sorry … *who?*"

CHAPTER 8

A FEW MORE SURPRISES

A FTER A WEEK James was allowed to pet the rescued cat, which seemed a lot brighter and had become quite playful. He had to ensure he returned her to Operations every evening, when he went to bed, though.

"What will we do with her when she's all better, Grandma?" James asked.

"We'll take her to the RSPCA and they'll find her a nice owner, don't worry."

They did exactly that the following Monday morning. Grandma spoke to the lady at the desk.

"As I explained on the phone," she said, "I think she's a stray. She just keeps turning up. I thought maybe you could check for one of those microtag thingys?"

The lady took the little cat away and returned after a moment saying,

"No, no micro-chip, madam. But if you're sure you don't want her, we'll keep her here. She's a nice little cat. We'll have no trouble finding a home."

When they were outside again, James spoke up.

"But didn't you *know* Grandma? That she didn't have a microchip?"

"Yes dear," Grandma said, "but, remember? I can't tell people what we do. So it was easier to just say she was a stray."

James nodded but asked:

"Won't they think it's funny - that she's had an operation?"

"Maybe … They'll notice some scarring, but they might just think it's from a fight. They certainly won't think the old lady who brought her in did it!"

James was very quiet on the bus ride home, with the empty cat carrier. He had enjoyed checking on her each day and, despite Grandma warning him not to get "attached", had come to think of the little cat as his second pet. Grandma interrupted his thoughts, speaking up over the noise of the engine and other passengers.

"So, young Jimmy-lad. How about helping Grandad with a project now? How are you with computers?"

James felt a little twinge of excitement in his tummy. "Is it the animals?"

"Yes," Grandma agreed, "time we checked up on a few."

James twisted around in his seat to better talk with his Grandma and decided today had improved quite a lot.

Evie's Monday morning had gone from odd, to very odd indeed. Left speechless by Kath's question about Artemis, Evie had sat dumbly, waiting for help. Maybe it was a huge coincidence, and one of the Spar staff was called … Artemis? Though why Evie should have met her already was anyone's guess. As the silence lengthened, Kath tried again.

"Artemis dear. She ought to have visited you? Over the weekend?"

"Ah," Evie replied, nodding very slowly. Then she had a flash of inspiration. "Sorry, what does – er, Artemis, er, look like, again?"

Kath frowned. "Well - medium sized, grey as I recall … green eyes maybe? Or yellow, I'm not really sure – "

Yellow, thought Evie.

"She's a *cat*." Evie said aloud.

Kath paused, studying Evie's face. "Yes … And she's called *Artemis*." Kath was talking more deliberately now, carefully pronouncing each word. "She *did* visit you, then …?"

Evie suddenly realised that she was not quite making the impression she had hoped.

"Yeah," she said, with a small smile.

"Ah, good." Kath sat down opposite, placed her hands on her knees and leaned forwards. "I could be wrong about this," she continued, "but I'm getting the feeling you may not be - *fully* informed?" Kath sighed and straightened her apron. "Communications! The bugbear of every organisation. Were you expecting to work at the Spar, by any chance? Level 2 Customer Service - behind the tills, stocking the shelves, bit of admin?"

"Well … yes," Evie whispered. Cat problems aside, she really needed a job. Had she blown it already?

"Ah." Kath had plonked a mug of tea on the table in front of Evie while they spoke and now pushed a little bowl of sugar sachets in Evie's direction. "Artemis shot off a bit quick, did she?" Evie nodded. "I see ... You'll have a few more questions that I thought then."

"I'm sorry," said Evie, "but, well, you ... you know about Artemis? And that she's a cat? And that, well, she can talk, then? And – so, if I'm not here for a job. Please - can you tell me why I *am* here? Or – " Evie's eyes started to feel hot and prickly. "Or is this, like, some massive *joke* or something?"

"Oh dear," Kath said, "have a sip of tea, love. This is going to take a little while, I think ... I'll just let Ayaan know."

Kath hopped up from her seat and disappeared into the shop for a moment. Evie sipped her tea then put it down and began picking at the edge of the table where the surface was chipped. She took long, slow breaths – conscious of feeling shaky inside – until Kath returned to settle into an easy chair, drink her tea, and talk.

"We've known about you for some time," Kath said. As she spoke she gestured freely with her hands, the mug hovering here and there yet not a drop spilled. "News gets around, on the grapevine, you know. Obviously I couldn't tell your *Matron*, bless her!" Kath chuckled, as if this were an in-joke and took a mouthful of tea. Evie smiled weakly and Kath continued:

"I *like* running the Spar. Suits me at my age, been an operative for *years*. Then I got this promotion to Co-Ord. Well, I like meeting people –" Evie pulled her smile a bit bigger at the corners, feeling as if she had joined a conversation half way through and was waiting for it all to make sense. "Look at *you*, just starting up like that, on the doorstep – well! We reckoned it was best you came here – to Lifelink? That's us – and it's you, too, if you like!"

Evie scanned the back room of the Spar. There didn't seem to be anything unusual about it: faded notices on a cork board, shabby furnishings, a computer at the desk. She realised Kath was watching her when a rich giggle burst from Kath's pillar-box red lips.

"It's not just the *Spar*, love. Lifelink's a whole organisation. A big one at that. Spar manager, well, it's a job – of course it is – but it's also cover. A shop's a good place to meet up and chat. You get all sorts in Spars."

Evie tried to concentrate harder.

"Anyway, so we knew you could speak, well hear, anyway. Don't think you knew you could though?

Not till Artemis popped in, eh? It's a funny old thing, creaturespeak, no rhyme nor reason to it sometimes. You can't always speak to everyone. Just have to give it a go. See, me, I'm only dogs! Best one though, dogs ... Not surprised that cat let us down. No empathy, cats, I don't trust them, not as far as - as I can swing 'em!"

Evie nodded in agreement, as she thought it best. Kath suddenly sat still and placed her hands, still holding her empty mug, on her knees.

"So anyway, we looked into your history, of course. Sad that. No family and all ..." She paused, then shrugged a little and carried on, "but, to be honest, it works for us. If you want it to, anyway... ideal recruit, at your age."

Evie, who felt the vaguest grasp of understanding forming in her mind like shapes made of smoke, took a breath, and asked:

"Er, Kath, sorry but I – er, recruit, to do what exactly? Please?" She added the 'please' hastily, suddenly remembering that there was still a minute possibility that the lady before her was in fact her future boss.

"To speak! We need people who can convey messages, make sure the right species get to communicate. And if you manage that – messages and the like – well, the sky's the limit really. We can train you up, you see. The details are all a bit Top Secret," she giggled briefly, stopped herself, and carried on, "so I can't go into them. But we have enemies. Well, who doesn't?"

Evie opened her mouth and breathed in, but closed it again.

"And we need more like you, multiple speakers, to gain information. So, I mean it's up to you, but you *could* train for that - be an agent, work in intelligence, that sort of thing. But only if you want to of course. It's not for everyone. Not my cup of tea!" Kath indicated her empty mug, placing it on the table. "So. What do you think? About the job dear! It's just probationary at first of course. *Probationary Operative* … Ah, those were the days." Kath plonked both hands down on her thighs with a slap. "Either way, I promised your Matron you'd have a job. You can still go on the checkout, glad of the help. Pay's about the same to be honest." She turned down one corner of her mouth as an apology, then stood up as the phone began to shrill loudly.

Funny old day, Evie thought as she waited. *Let's see … checkouts … Or … secret agent? Checkouts, or … Hah!*

CHAPTER 9

LIFELINK AND CREATURESPEAK

JAMES AND GRANDAD were sitting side-by-side at the Ops room computer, logged into software called "EagleView", that recorded the movements of all the creatures that had had implants from Grandma. It basically showed a series of maps with coloured dots, each colour representing a different type of animal. Cats were red, dogs blue, birds yellow. There were a lot more colours.

To James, for someone who couldn't 'get the hang of those electrical game things' Grandad seemed suspiciously fast with a keyboard, not to mention the touchscreen. He thought there was a lot of stuff Grandad had been keeping quiet.

"Grandad," James queried, "what are the light purple ones?"

A couple of lilac dots meandered around onscreen about ten miles away.

"Hm?" Grandad responded absently. "Light purple? Oh, yes. They're horses. Now, if you see over here - "

"*Horses?*" James echoed loudly. "Does Grandma bring *horses* here, to Ops?"

Grandad coughed, before turning to give James his full attention.

"Sorry Jimmy, I was forgetting … well … who I was with, to be honest. Actually, Grandma does - what you might call - 'house calls,' sometimes. Like a regular vet. To some, er, special customers."

"Like who?"

"Like, other agents."

"So … other agents own horses? And, did they get sick then?"

Grandad's forehead creased up and he called out loudly, making James jump:

"Em! Come here a minute will you?"

Mr T had hopped up on the chair next to him and James began stroking his neck. Mr T purred loudly.

"Getting in a bit of a pickle Agent Zed? I *could* say I told you so." Mr T was thoroughly enjoying being able to criticise Zed with James in the room. If Zed responded, James would surely want to know who he was speaking to and another secret would be out. Zed carefully scooped Mr T off the chair, saying to James:

"Think I'll just sit down for a moment, while your Grandma explains."

James looked up to see Grandma come in, drying her hands on a tea-towel.

"What's the problem then boys?" she said.

"Jimmy's wondering about the horses ..." Grandad began.

"Horses?"

"Mm," said Grandad. "He was wondering, how you, er, came to put EagleView chips - in the horses. I told him. You do some work. For other agents -"

"Yes," chimed in James. "I didn't know there were other agents so near! How many are there? Do they all do what you and Grandad do? Although they can't, can they – I mean, if they need you to be their vet? So do you treat all their pets? And – what do the other agents do then?"

"Goodness me!" said Grandma, though she was smiling now. "You, young man, have a lot of questions!"

"You *told* me so?" Grandad said, oddly.

"Sorry, Grandad?" said James.

Grandad shook his head. Grandma ignored him and carried on speaking.

"I'm glad you're sitting down dear. I've one or two things to explain. The horses there, and the other dots too come to that - they're actually not pets. They don't *belong* to agents. Those dots - they *are* the agents."

"But, they're animals, Grandma." James giggled.

"Yes," agreed Grandma, "and agents."

Twenty minutes later James decided the world was getting stranger and stranger. He had just listened to his grandparents explain between them that there were some people who could understand what animals were saying. And that some of the animals could talk back, using 'creaturespeak'. Also, that there were people like his grandparents working for Lifelink all over the world tracking animal agents, so they could be contacted whenever the organisation needed them. His grandparents had stopped talking after delivering this information and both sat facing James. He felt they were now waiting for him to say something.

"Grandma," James said.

"Yes, dear?"

"That's just … *mad*."

"He doesn't believe us," Grandad said.

"You can't blame him. It's pretty far-fetched when you think about it. We're used to it. We grew up with it. But we've just sprung it on him … out of nowhere." Grandma nodded, though in the direction of Mr T. "Jimmy darling, I'm going to phone your Mum. I think we should visit her. I've rather overstepped a promise just now and, before I make it even worse, I need to see your Mum. Will you wait while I phone?"

Grandad stared at James, before making a "hmph" noise, then turning back to the screen and flicking between menus.

James went over to the little sofa, grabbing Mr T by the middle on the way. He tickled him under the chin, then held up his head and peered deeply into Mr T's eyes. He whispered to his cat.

"Mr T, I think my grandparents are … a bit mad. They're very old, you know. And that can happen when you get very old. I'm glad I'm going to see Mum today." He considered for a moment. "It *would* be cool though, wouldn't it? If you could talk to me?"

"Indeed," Mr T purred, while James continued to scratch under Mr T's chin.

"You're my best friend, Mr T," said the boy.

"And you are mine, James," said Mr T, still purring – the one way he could actually communicate with the boy. He settled himself down, padding his paws into the sofa cushion, to wait for Agent Em's return. Mr T was good at waiting.

James ran towards his Mum's bed when they reached the ward. She was sitting in a chair beside it with a cup of coffee, which she carefully placed on the table as he landed for a hug.

"Mum!" James was thinking she looked like her old self again.

"Oh, it's good to see you," Mum gave him the big smile that made her eyes shine. She also gave him a squeeze and patted the mattress beside her chair. He jumped up to sit next to her.

"Helen, we'll just, er, go and … grab a cup of coffee, shall we?" Grandad muttered from over by the bed screen.

"That would probably be a good idea," Mum said. Grandma swept Grandad out of the ward ahead of her.

"Mum," James jumped straight in, as he wasn't sure how long he had before his grandparents' return. "I'm worried about Grandad and Grandma. I think - I think they're - imagining things. They're kind of *old* you know, and they're telling me stuff that … well, it isn't *real*."

Mum was quiet for a few seconds.

"I know, James," she smiled, but a bit sadly James thought. She must be worried about them too. "Stories about animals that can talk?"

"That's it!" James said, happy she already knew. "Did Grandma tell you too?"

"James," Mum paused, and he waited, giving her hand a little squeeze of sympathy. "James …

Grandma didn't have to tell me. I already knew."
James, shocked, let go of her hand without thinking.
If Mum had known his grandparents were ill, why
had she sent him to stay with them? He waited for
an explanation. "Sweetheart, I'm your *Mum*. You
do trust me? Don't you?"

"Yes, of course Mum." James waited again.

"There's nothing wrong with your grandparents."

"No, there is Mum. You don't understand. They were
telling me that people could talk to animals. And that
animals were, well, were *secret agents*, and all sorts
of stuff. But – it was like they *really* meant it, Mum.
Like, for them, it wasn't just, a story – "

"No, it wasn't just a story. And not just to them."
James took a sharp breath up through his nose and
his Mum reached out for his hand. "James, have I
ever lied to you?"

"No, of course not."

"Well, then … Look. Do you remember - when we
planted the apple pips? When you were four?" James
did, though he had no idea why Mum was bringing
it up now. "And, after a while, little trees grew up
in the pot. And I explained, how they had come
from the pips? Do you remember how amazed you
were? Then we planted them in the garden and that

little tree in the corner, that's the one that survived? James, sweetheart, do you remember you thought it was magic?"

"Ye-es…" James was about to say that that was not the same thing at all, but Mum went on.

"Well, as you grow up, you discover a lot of things. And some of them can seem - pretty strange. But you have to ask someone, someone who already knows, to explain it to you. That's when you believe it, properly. Mostly, at your age, we learn things when we're ready. We have lessons, and we're, prepared." Mum cupped her other hand around his too and leaned forward. "But not always. James, you have just learned something you were not ready for. I am not crazy, and your grandparents are not crazy. But we do have a secret. And it's one I actually didn't want you to learn. Not until you had to, anyway. And maybe not ever."

Mum paused and reached for the plastic glass with water in it. James searched around in his brain for a sentence, for a thought that summed up what he had just heard. He came up with *My grandparents are not crazy*.

He searched for something to attach to that and found *They told me animals can talk to people*. He realised his mouth was dry too, stuck shut, so he swallowed. Then opened it to speak.

Then closed it again.

Then opened it. Then spoke.

"Mum …? Do *you* believe in, in the animals thing, too?"

"No James, I don't *believe in* it." James opened his mouth yet again, but Mum carried on. "I *know* it. For a fact. Now, I have asked your Grandma to prove it to you. This afternoon. But I wanted the chance to talk to you first. There's something I wanted to tell you myself ... Your Dad - he could speak with animals, too. A lot of animals. Because of that, well, it's certainly possible at any rate - that you will, too."

James blinked and stared at Mum. He felt weird, a bit dizzy.

"But, I can't, Mum. Animals don't - talk to me." Inside his head, James heard how odd this sentence sounded. Mum, who had been frowning until now, laughed quietly.

"Not yet, maybe. And maybe not ever. But you're only eleven. A bit early. Wait a year or two, and we'll know then."

A year or two! James' head was at once full of thoughts again. Part of him didn't believe any of this. Part of him knew Mum always told him the truth. Part of him was scared of the whole idea. And part of him wanted desperately for it to be true. But all of him was absolutely sure he didn't want to wait two whole years to find out!

"I have to wait *two* years? What am I going to *do* for two years?"

"I see you're partly convinced anyway! But you don't have to wait two years for proof of creaturespeak. Your grandparents can show you that." James' Mum gave him another big hug and looked up over his shoulder.

His grandparents were standing quietly near the doorway and she beckoned them across. James didn't know how long they'd been there. Had they heard him tell Mum they were losing their minds? He felt his neck glowing pink under his ginger hair.

"So, Jimmy-lad." Grandad dropped a heavy, calloused hand onto his shoulder. "Ready to go? We didn't quite finish your lesson, if you recall. Also …" He chuckled. "I've been waiting a long time for a good reason to make that cat want to follow orders." Adding, confusingly: "Hey, Em - do you think he can stand on his head yet?"

CHAPTER 10

BEG~~INNINGS~~

E VIE RECEIVED A text from Kath, instructing her to meet a Lifelink mentor in the park the following day at ten o'clock. She arrived at the bench by the pond, as instructed. After five minutes or so of sitting there, she was getting impatient, when a deep voice spoke - quite loudly - directly behind her.

"My new student, I presume?"

Evie, startled, whipped her head round and saw empty sky. In the next instant, she lowered her gaze, to look straight into the deep brown, amused eyes of a waist-high mountain of black-and-brown fur, with a bar of white straight down the middle of her face. Her wide, doggy smile appeared to be laughing at Evie, whose own mouth was hanging open, with nothing to say.

"First lesson. Always keep your wits about you. I'm Agent Loulou."

After this introduction, and a stroll around the park together, Loulou had just sort of moved into Evie's flat: a flat which seemed extremely small suddenly, full to the brim with Bernese Mountain dog.

Loulou didn't seem to mind. She had repositioned the sofa cushions onto the floor and requested that Evie pop to the Spar for a couple of suitable dinner bowls and some cans of dog food: "the good stuff, if you don't mind. Kath will know."

Evie herself was constantly expecting an irate landlord to knock on the door and remind her that the No Pets policy most definitely included very large dogs. When she timidly voiced this possibility, Loulou reminded Evie that she was, in fact, a house guest – not a pet - and that should it become problematic she could easily depart. But, for now, it was convenient to be near her student so she could constantly impart knowledge.

Evie had to admit it suited her admirably too. Never one for too much conversation, she found the perfect match in Loulou, who almost never stopped telling her things. Her deep, round-toned, rumble of a voice quietly filled Evie's head with stories of the past and the present.

"As far as we know there has never been a time when people and animals have not been able to talk to each other but, as the world grew more sophisticated, fewer and fewer people seemed to possess the ability. There were of course groups of humans all over the world who retained it better than others: native Americans, Maoris, some Pagans in Britain. Quite naturally, these were people who built their lives around animals, plants, the Earth. Their concerns were much more attuned to organic life than those whose central focus was, for instance, making money."

Loulou shifted on the cushions, heaving her bulky chest to one side and plummeting down again to lean on her paws, her head raised a little to speak.

"Not to say that it is as simple as that: Lifelink has human engineers and bankers within our organisation, and far from all the world's secluded human tribes can still creaturespeak. It's rather a random talent I'm afraid. But the real worry is that it's growing less common generally, as the years go by. The family lines nowadays tend to be few and well known."

Evie was perched on the edge of the cushionless settee. She watched Loulou haul her torso upright, to meet Evie's gaze head on.

"Finding a brand-new speaker, like yourself, is exciting news! It must have been a difficult thing to discover, surrounded by non-speakers like that. In the past, speakers in your position have been labelled as having some type of delusion and usually given medication to stop them hearing 'the voices', meaning we lost them before we had chance to intervene."

Evie pondered silently on her decision, nearly five years previously, to keep her voices a secret. If not for that, she would never have known about any of this. Loulou was still talking though.

"But speakers who are lucky enough to grow up in a creaturespeaking family, well they almost always become Lifelink members. A few are what we call 'neutrals' – they don't really want to be involved. And fewer still become – well, we'll come to that. But all of us – whatever our beliefs - keep creaturespeak secret from the non-speakers. Because frankly, historically, humans are always afraid of things they can't understand."

"But why do we need an organisation?" said Evie. "What's if *for?* I mean, it's not just a club, is it - it has agents?"

"Yes," Loulou shifted, then stood up and paced around the living room. It didn't take her long. "Evie, not all animals are as pleasant as me."

Evie giggled. Loulou was many things - stern, talkative, full of information, *big*. 'Pleasant' just wasn't the first word to spring to mind.

Loulou sat back on her haunches again, facing Evie, who was now sitting cross-legged.

"Not the best response," Loulou huffed. "What I am trying to say is that not everyone likes humans. You seem to be able to communicate with a lot of species, really a phenomenal talent, but not everyone you speak to will *want* you to understand them. There are a number of creatures capable of communicating with humans who choose not to, if they can help it."

"And is that a problem?" responded Evie. "I mean, I should have thought it was up to them. Their loss."

"And you would be right, if it were only that simple. There is a reason many refuse to communicate and it is the very same reason the rest of us *do* speak. Those speakers who do not join Lifelink may or may not join the group we call *Misants*. Misants believe that humans have ruined the Earth..."

"Oh," Evie said, adding: "but I suppose they're right in a way. I mean we have, haven't we? You know, rain forests and stuff."

"That's very honest of you Evie. A good response. Yes, you have. But that destruction is *all* the Misants see. There are those of us, however, who think more deeply than that. Mankind is also involved in some very courageous endeavours." Evie gave a small smile, feeling quite grateful for some reason.

"Lifelink's view is that we are where we are, today. There have been mistakes in the past, certainly, made by humans and catastrophic for the planet we all share. But other humans have recognised that now, and they are trying to repair it. These people are *precious* to us."

Evie tried to think of good things that mankind did. Loulou was helping out, however.

"There are people trying to rebuild populations of Sumatran tigers and Leatherback turtles. People trying to stop deforestation. People wanting to repair and rebuild our planet. The Lifelink view is that we *need* humans, in order to accomplish the planet's restoration. We need your technology, your dexterity, your ideas, to put things right - and we believe more and more of you are understanding this." Loulou edged a little closer and Evie felt the warmth of Loulou's breath as she almost growled at her: "Evie, just imagine an increasing number of people all trying to put the world *right! That's* Lifelink's dream."

"What's the Misants' dream?" Evie whispered. Loulou flopped back down, the energy gone out of her.

"That humans as we know you today cease to exist. That you give up all scientific and technological endeavour and return to a stone-age lifestyle … *or* that you simply die out. They have no strong preference. If you could leave on a rocket ship I am sure that would do just as well. Remove modern-day humans and the world will gradually right itself."

Evie did not reply. She felt as if something had clawed its way down her spine, and shivered realising she was nauseous.

"I'm sorry," said Loulou. "I could probably have done that better. Kath would have done it better." Loulou stood up and paced the room once more. "I forget how it must feel for you. For us it's old news. It's just why we do what we do, to prevent the Misants achieving their aims so we can allow mankind time to change its ways and repair the world."

"Loulou?" Evie's mouth was dry. She swallowed and tried again. "Loulou, how do the Misants expect that this, any of the stuff they want to happen, will happen? What do they … do?"

"Shall we go for a walk?"

Evie, startled, nodded and jumped up, leaving the flat to follow her tutor along the road to the park.

Once they had walked between the rusty old gates and reached the downward sloping expanse of grass, bordered with trees, Loulou's mood appeared to brighten as she lifted her nose to sniff in great gulps of fresh air.

"Evie, it's not all bad." Loulou's growly voice sounded warm to Evie, like a smile. "But the Misants do whatever they can. To get in the way of humanity - to foil your projects - and, sadly, there are of course humans who help them."

"*People?*" Evie was astonished. "*Why* would people help?"

"Greed." Loulou said. "It's a long-term project Evie. If it worked, it would take a good few of your generations. It *has* taken a good few. A lot of humans just don't think beyond their own lives, don't ever look beyond themselves. If helping the Misants can make them rich, perhaps by taking out their opposition, or securing funding to develop viruses, or by being paid to fight, or set bombs, well - they don't care about the consequences. As long as they won't be the ones to suffer. Which is ironic, really."

"Is it?"

"It is if you think of the sorts of humans who brought about this mess. Their greed, their selfishness. Ironic that the Misants should allow the same types of humans to help them out now …. I believe there are also a few who actually believe in the Misants' cause, though - that you *should* all go back to nature ... So anyway - yes, Misants have help. But," she added in a low growl, "that still doesn't mean they'll succeed."

The two walked on, in silence, Evie pondering how humans could be so evil that they could even try to profit from their planet dying. Loulou, padding along heavily beside her, suddenly began speaking again - starting with a small "woof" that dragged Evie's attention back to the present.

"Misants are *disorganised* though. There are far fewer of them than there are Lifelink members. They tend to be fanatical. If they all acted together then they might be more of a force to reckon with but, at the moment, their goal is a very long way off. It's Lifelink's job to keep it that way." Loulou brushed against Evie's side; she felt solid, warm. "We want to stop them hurting anyone, sure, but the best result would be to convince them that we can work *together* to achieve a balanced world. Prevention and Conversion. Lifelink will train you to go out in the field and do this work. But it can be dangerous."

Loulou had stopped walking and Evie turned around to see why.

"There are creatures out there, Evie – animal and human – who will stop you doing your job *by any means*. You need to really understand that before you finally commit to the life. Kath will need to tell HQ soon, whether or not you're up for becoming a field agent."

"I am." Evie had barely let Loulou finish her sentence.

"Just hold on!" Loulou's voice bubbled up from deep inside her, like laughter Evie thought. "That's great, but you haven't thought about it long enough. It's not just this week or next we're talking about, Evie. Once you're in, you're in. This job becomes your whole way of life. There are other roles you could undertake, ones that still help Lifelink."

Evie took a breath. She wanted to say this right.

"Agent Loulou, I have thought about it. That's what I've been doing, since you said 'humans have ruined the Earth.' I get how the Misants must feel and why they must hate us. As for me, I don't have anyone to worry about except myself, so who better to worry about the whole of humanity and get involved, even if it's dangerous? Except it's not just humanity of course. There's no separating humans and other species, or the planet itself for that matter. I think Misants are wrong in what they want, but they're right too, that the world needs fixing. They should be stopped, because I can't see how more destruction can be the answer. We'd lose all the good stuff as well as the bad. Surely it's as wrong for the Misants to hurt and destroy humans, as it is for us to hurt and destroy others? Don't you think?"

Evie stopped and sucked in a breath.

Loulou had been standing very still, listening to Evie without blinking.

"Evie," Loulou said. "You're in." She padded over and shoved her nose briefly into one of Evie's hands, then turned away and headed towards the Spar.

To Evie's surprise, Loulou didn't say anything more.

After that conversation, Evie found herself spending all her waking hours with her canine teacher, most of them roaming the parks and streets as Loulou could not be cooped up in the flat too long. Evie lived in her trainers, carrying their food in her backpack, and was pleased to realise she felt stronger and fitter than ever. As they walked, Loulou talked.

Evie found herself learning about all sorts of subjects - like history, a class she had dropped like a hot brick five years ago. But this wasn't the dreary recollection of battles, dates and kings she remembered from school. This was stuff that mattered: the history of creaturespeak, the creation of Lifelink, and then the emergence of Misants.

The same for geography: no more ox-bows and meanders, but a general knowledge of places in the world where Lifelink had a presence. Then there was politics: not a subject she had ever studied or even considered before. This was the most difficult: who could speak with whom; who *would* speak with whom; and what they each wanted and believed.

Cats and dogs, she knew, were the easiest creatures to speak with: animals that had been domesticated, living alongside mankind for thousands of years. They could also almost always understand each other too. Next came horses, which was hardly surprising. Loulou had asked Evie what other animals she thought might be easily understood.

She considered for a moment, then said:

"Cows. And sheep!"

Loulou laughed, well, barked – but it sounded like she was laughing, to Evie.

"That would be exactly what I expected you to say," Loulou said, "but not so."

Evie was pouting slightly at Loulou's amusement.

"Well, what then?"

"Oh come on, cheer up – it's not so obvious I suppose. Cows and sheep are actually really hard to read – and pigs – any farm animals really. They've been around people for a long time, I grant you, but not so much part of human lives. Plus …" Loulou made a huffing noise. "We think they're just - wired differently. You won't like this distinction much, but animals that hunt and live in packs, they tend to be understood. And the others – what you might call natural prey – not so much. I'm sorry if that offends you."

"I'm not offended!" Evie laughed, "I'm not a vegetarian!"

"So – do you know what the answer is then?"

Evie considered.

"Yes – I do – it's birds, isn't it?"

"Not bad! It is - *some* birds, yes."

Evie furrowed her brow. Some birds. To be honest she'd been going to suggest budgerigars or parrots – they were always around people after all.

"Oh – I know!" Evie felt a flush of excitement. "Hawks! It's hawks, isn't it – birds of prey. I'm right. Am I?"

Loulou shoved Evie's right hand in a gesture Evie had come to value as approval.

"Yes, indeed you are. Hawks, falcons – mankind has been hunting with them for years. They understand each other pretty well."

Evie had a sudden thought.

"But horses – horses don't hunt things!"

"No, I know. As I said, it's complex. Horses don't hunt – well, not without a rider anyway - but they have been one with man a long time. And they're big."

"Big?"

"Mm. Big. Larger animals have a better chance of being speakers than small ones."

"But not cows."

"But not cows." Loulou produced what Evie took to be the doggy version of a chuckle. "As I said, it's complex. And the only way to find out who can speak with you, is to try it."

They had been walking for the entire lesson and Loulou came to an abrupt halt.

"In you go," she said. The sign over the big open gates ahead said *Zoo*. Evie had not been paying attention to their surroundings during the conversation.

"What? On my own?"

Loulou stared at her for a long moment until Evie blushed, realising that the zoo was unlikely to welcome canine visitors.

"Sorry," she muttered. "So – what do I do?"

"Try it out," replied Loulou. "Subtly, I would suggest. I'll be back here when it closes."

Evie watched Loulou trot off along the pavement, disappearing quickly between two houses, presumably not wanting to attract too much stray-dog attention. Determinedly, Evie took out her wallet and entered the zoo.

CHAPTER 11

CONVERSATIONS

JAMES WAS IN the living room of 45 Cromwell Street, watching while Grandad spoke directly to Mr T - who clearly understood everything said to him. Grandad asked Mr T to walk around the room, jump up on a chair, lie down, then stand up. Finally he asked him to roll onto his back and have a tummy tickle. At that point Mr T had sat resolutely still, gazing, unblinking at Grandad. Grandad chuckled.

"Seems I've hit my limit here Jimmy. Mr T says 'no'. I'm guessing the headstand's out then?"

Mr T stalked away, then changed his mind and sat on the sofa near James instead, who whispered, his voice shaking a little:

"Mr T, can you understand me too?"

"He says 'yes'."

This was Grandma, as she entered the room.

James blinked rapidly, and he felt a strong grip tighten for a split second on his chest, as he suddenly fully understood what had just happened.

As long as he had had him, James had talked to Mr T.

He had told him all the annoyances at school and at home, his hopes, his dreams, and his nightmares. He had confessed to Mr T when he had been naughty and complained to Mr T when he had been told off. He had shared happy moments with Mr T too, of course. James suddenly realised that this cat knew more about him than anyone else on the planet, including his own Mum. James' tummy felt odd and he folded his arms around it. When he did, Mr T edged closer to James, and pushed his head under James' hand, angling for a stroke behind the ears just like he always did.

Grandma came over to perch next to James and placed her warm hand on his arm.

"You need to remember, Jimmie dear, that Mr T is still your cat. For that matter, you're still his boy. Mr T hasn't changed at all. He's part of the family now, and he's still just as fussy and needy and annoying as he ever was." Mr T gave Grandma a look. "Mr T has always had a voice – you just didn't know. He's no different, and he certainly wouldn't have stuck around now if he wasn't very attached to you, and your Mum."

James nodded. He was very grateful to Grandma for understanding. He tried to get his head around the fact that nothing had really changed – not for Mr T at least.

For James, however, it had changed quite a lot. Knowing Mr T could understand what he said was something he was just going to have to accept, but knowing he could not understand Mr T - that was maddening. It just didn't seem fair.

"Grandma, how long before I can understand cats?" James had not taken his eyes off Mr T while they spoke.

"Oh, now." Grandma ruffled James' hair. "We can't rush these things. Talents tend to develop when children hit their teens. Some are a bit earlier, some are quite late indeed. The odds are good - because of your Dad, and Grandad and myself - but there's no guarantee. It can even skip a generation or three. But you shouldn't be worrying yourself about that just yet, it's far too early."

James heard the words "it can even skip a generation" and fell silent, until Grandad broke through his thoughts.

"Come on then, let's hit that computer! We barely scratched the surface yesterday. You've a lot to learn young man, assuming you still want to?"

James did! He gave Mr T a friendly stroke and jumped up to follow Grandad into Ops, all other worries pushed to the back of his mind for today.

"Em," purred Mr T.

"Mm?"

"He's in now, isn't he, hrrr?"

"Yes, T," Agent Em said. "I rather think he is. He's young though. The same age his Dad was when we first took him out." Agent Em's face fell for a moment, then she shook her head and stood purposefully up. "You're really very fond of that boy, aren't you … Mr T? That's good. There was a time I didn't think you had a thoughtful bone in your body, you know."

"Was there? Don't think I've gone soft, Agent Em. It's just - listening to the hopes and fears of a child over the years … it's a window to their soul. Hrrr. It's a good soul, Em. It's one we want involved." Mr T stretched as he stood up. "I know he's just a child now, but what is this all about if not the future, hrrr? You and I won't live to see it, but *he* might. I think he's important, Em - and not just to us."

"I know, T. I think he has skills he has yet to realise. If only because he dragged *you* out from behind that mask of indifference."

"Hrrr. It's not a mask, Em. It's armour, in this job." Mr T padded away towards Ops, thinking of other agents he could never see again.

James had fallen into bed at 9.00 pm, his brain buzzing with all the information Grandad had shown him in Ops. One part of the system they had not touched, was just called "Tasking." James had asked what it was – it sounded like a list of jobs.

"Yes it is, sort of," Grandad agreed. "But they're very special jobs. We call them missions."

James had wanted to see the mission screens but Grandad had said that 'unfortunately access' was 'limited.' What missions could possibly involve a network of *animal* agents? He could not begin to imagine.

James slept that night with his head full of maps, names of Ops stations, lists of animals. He dreamed he was one of the agents, a kestrel flying through the night with important information; next he was running along the pavement with a cat's-eye view of the world, intent on a secret destination. When he woke, it took him a moment to leave his dreams behind and stumble downstairs, to find his own very special creature agent, waiting patiently in the kitchen for breakfast.

"Morning, Mr T," said James aloud, as he did every morning.

"Morning James," said Mr T, as he always did even if James didn't know it, winding round James' ankle, following it with his customary: "Sleep well, hrrr?"

"I had crazy dreams," James said, rubbing the side of his nose.

Mr T's eyes narrowed.

"James?" meowed Mr T, sharply.

"Yes?" said James, then dropped the packet of cat food – smack! - on the floor, letting his mouth drop open about as wide as it possibly could.

"Hah!" cried Mr T, with an ear-splitting yowl that made James just about the happiest he had ever felt.

Later that same day James ran through the hospital ward straight to Mum's bed, calling out:

"Mum, I have news!"

Mum, who was standing beside the bed, leaning on a crutch, beamed right back at him.

"So have I James – the doctor says I'm doing really well and I can go home! They're discharging me tomorrow. You can come home, James love!"

James stopped still, and his arms fell limp at his sides.

"Oh. Oh, that's … great Mum. Really good -" he said.

"What was your news, sweetheart?"

James answered, quietly.

"I can do it, Mum. I can speak. It happened this morning. I'm like Dad - and I can speak to cats."

"Oh," said Mum. "That's … that's early. You must be really pleased."

"Yeah …"

To James' relief, a nurse came into the ward apologising for interrupting the visit, saying the doctor was ready to assess Mrs Doughty, if now would be convenient?

"Oh yes, of course," said Mum in response, turning to James to add: "Shall you go back and find Grandad, James? We'll talk in a little while?"

James nodded and meandered back towards the elevator.

He pictured himself minutes before, running down the stairs, flying ahead of his grandparents in order to tell Mum the exciting news. Now he felt like a popped balloon inside. He watched the elevator doors open and his grandparents stepped out behind a man in blue scrubs. James told them the doctor was with Mum, and they had to wait, turning to head towards the café as he did so.

"Jimmy? Hold up," called Grandad. "Did you tell her yet?"

James slowed down and turned. He studied Grandad's face, its forehead furrowed, its eyes hawk-like.

"I did. Grandad, Mum's better. She's going home." He looked from Grandad to Grandma, searching for Grandma's expression behind the reflections in her glasses. "Grandma, I'm going home."

Evie noisily filled the kettle as Kath plonked herself down on one of the kitchen chairs. Evie clicked the switch then turned around, leaning against the sink. There was a "hrmph" noise of air being breathed out in the next room and an impatient thump of a tail on the carpet.

"So, how was it?" Kath said.

"Not really how I thought," said Evie at last.

"Oh?"

"I'm not sure *what* I thought. I just wandered around, and anytime it was quiet, I said 'hi'."

"Hi?"

"Not *just* 'hi'. I said my name, and I asked if they could speak. Some of them did." Evie stumbled on. "But most of them didn't. I don't know if they couldn't, or if they were just ignoring me. I mean, how do you tell?"

"How indeed," Kath muttered.

"So anyway, loads didn't speak, but the hyenas did, first."

"Much?"

"Not really. They asked me what I was doing there. Was I mocking them? They weren't very nice to be honest, not much of a laugh. And the gorillas, they were the same. *Who sent me? Didn't I know gorillas were impartial?* They asked me to move on and leave them in peace. I don't know, I just thought they'd be - *nicer*."

There was a deep-throated chuckle from the living room.

"Yes, I'm sorry, you probably did." Kath said. "It's good for you to try speaking, but it's not so interesting for them. The zoo is useful – lots of species in one place. But of course it's a zoo. The animals in there – they're not typical. Some of them want to be there, some of them – like the hyenas I'm guessing - don't. Most zoo animals are bred in captivity and they have a very narrow view of events. The world has never really affected them like it has us."

"Stockholm syndrome," said a gruff voice.

"Not necessarily, Loulou" said Kath. "They just don't know anything better. All they know is where and how they have always lived."

Loulou "hrmphed" and fell silent.

"So," said Kath. "Any more?"

"Yes," Evie brightened. "Owls. The owls were great."

"Really – in daytime?"

"Yes, I woke them up. They were all tucked up in the corners of the enclosures where it's dark and some were inside the little huts. No visitors around, because they were pretty boring, so I shouted at them."

Kath blinked, and Loulou poked her nose through the door. Evie grinned.

"Turns out, an irritated owl is a talkative owl! OK, at first it was mostly 'shut up' and 'what do you think you're doing?' But, when I explained, they were quite interested. I guess I probably did most of the talking when I think about it." Evie stood up straight now, keen to explain. "When I said why I was there, there was this really small owl – well, it would be I suppose - the sign said: 'Little Owl', so – but she said, 'Oh it's you.' And of course, I asked her what she meant, and then the Barn Owl said they'd already heard of me! Me! Apparently owls and bats can talk and they'd heard there was a new kid on the block, like, already. How cool is that?"

Kath had developed a half smile and was quietly nodding along with this last sentence.

"Pretty cool," she said. "The creaturespeak grapevine is good Evie. It's can be hard to keep a secret. You'd think, with all the confusion of species and languages, it would be easy, but somehow news always travels.

You need to remember that. It's wise to be careful what you discuss and where you discuss it."

"Yes, indeed," Loulou rumbled from the doorway. "When you said you did most of the talking – it was just about yourself, right?"

"Er, yes, I think so," Evie said, casting her mind back to the owl enclosure.

"Don't worry," Kath said. "You don't know any state secrets - yet. We wouldn't have sent you otherwise. Owls!" She chuckled. "It's true what they say – wise old birds. They get you to tell them everything and give nothing away. And they have memories like elephants. Did you know human scientists think that owls are quite dumb? They're brilliant actors, the lot of them. Never play poker with an owl!" Evie swallowed her tea quickly, about to speak. "Joke," said Kath, "They can't hold the cards ... What were you going to say?"

"Er," Evie thought again. "Well - what happens now?

"Now," Loulou said. "We go out in the field. I've been recalled to HQ. They have a job for me – nothing too dangerous I am assured - but I need a human partner, and I think it should be you."

Evie was stunned. Kath smirked and patted Evie on the arm.

"You're ready Evie. You've got to start somewhere. You couldn't have anyone better than Loulou to show you the ropes. Do you think you can get a few things together by morning? You'll have to travel light – just a backpack, I'm afraid."

Evie walked over to the tall cupboard that housed the ironing board and hauled out her beloved backpack.

"I've had this packed for a fortnight," she said, grinning shyly at Kath. "Just in case."

CHAPTER 12

CAT TROUBLE

JAMES AND GRANDAD were finishing up their sandwiches in the café while Grandma had headed off down a corridor to the wards, to see whether Mum was finished with the nurse yet. Grandad pushed his plate away, said that he could do with a cup of tea and asked if James wanted anything to drink.

"No, thanks, Grandad. Shall I go and find Grandma and ask her?"

"Good idea, ask your Mum too, she might prefer the coffee they do here. I'll just take a look at that cake …"

Grandad strode over to the counter, fishing in his jacket for his wallet, and James slid off his chair to head back towards the ward. He knew exactly where to go, they had spent so many hours here. He found the ward and saw Mum and Grandma chatting beside Mum's bed. There was only one other bed, which was empty, and James was about to call out to them when he noticed their faces - both of which were set in expressions of great seriousness. Not entirely sure why he did, James slipped behind the curtain that hid the empty bed and waited, listening.

"I wanted a word, just us," Grandma said.

She was standing near the end of Mum's bed.

James peered through a crack where the curtains met and watched as Mum patted the mattress. Grandma perched on the edge of it.

"Helen, what would you say to Jimmy staying with us for the next couple of weeks?" James sucked in a silent breath. "Think about it for a moment. I know you must miss him terribly, but you'll be hobbling around for a while yet and you need to be fully fit before school starts again. He's been loving the work, and he would never say, because he wouldn't want to upset you, but I'm absolutely sure he had hoped he'd be able to carry on with it, till he went back to school at least." Grandma was fiddling with a corner of the sheet and speaking quickly.

"Emma, I'm not an idiot."

James blinked and bit his lips together. Mum was staring at his Grandma, in a way James was not used to seeing. There was something about it that reminded him of the head mistress at school.

"No dear," Grandma said.

"I know James – *James* – " Mum repeated his name for some reason, "wants to work with you two. I also know *you* could imagine nothing better. He's your grandson, he's the family line, so of course you want him to stay. But I want you to realise something Emma. He is not, absolutely *not*, his father. James is *not* Jake. He is a little boy, just finished primary school, who has been brought up in an entirely different world - a normal world. He's half me. And, yes, he's half Jake. But as Jake is not here," she paused and studied Grandma. "I have the final say in what my son does, or does not, do. Right up until he's old enough to legally do that for himself."

"Of course, dear," Grandma said.

James felt his muscles tense up as he concentrated hard on not moving or breathing too loudly.

"I'm not finished," Mum added. Grandma tilted her chin, like she was asking a question. "As I said, I'm not an idiot. I wanted to see what his reaction would be – and I did."

Mum reached for the little cup of water by the bed and sipped it. His Grandma just waited, watching

Mum, and still holding the chunk of sheet tightly in her fist.

"I have been thinking about every aspect of this day since James was born. I have thought it through so many times, and every time I come up with the same plan, so I have stuck to it. The first phase was to shield my son from his father's world for as long as possible. Jake agreed to that you know." James became aware of his heart thumping hard, as if it wanted to give him away. "I wanted James to know other things. Jake was obsessed with Lifelink from the moment he began to think. I knew that of course, and I'm not complaining about his choices, but look at us now. He's gone Emma, and we don't know where or why. Lifelink is not a normal way of life for most people on the Earth – just for you guys. You can't blame me for wanting James to have some time out from it, at the start. I always knew if he began to creaturespeak he'd be lost to me. I made provision for it. I just haven't told him yet."

Grandma shook her head and leaned in a bit closer to Mum.

"What sort of provision, Helen?"

"For his education. You can take him with you sometimes, but his education continues. He does not just drop off the grid."

Take me with them? James thought, feeling confused.

"Helen, we don't want to take him away! He just wants to stay for the holidays!" Grandma protested.

"Oh, come *on*, Emma. What do you think will happen in September? Do you think he will magically return to school and everything will be forgotten – that he'll sit in Maths class concentrating on … trigonometry? Or do you think he'll be staring out of the window trying to catch a few words from the starlings on the roof, or planning his next visit to Ops, or wondering where you can take him at half term? How long before I start getting student concern emails and we're at loggerheads all the time? He hasn't even entered puberty yet but he's been set up for a running head start at being angry and repressed."

Mum stopped speaking, perhaps noticing that Grandma's face had sort of crumpled. James himself was finding it increasingly difficult to stay still behind his curtain, wanting nothing more than to run out and ask them what was happening.

"Helen, I'm sorry," Grandma whispered, her head lowered. "We, I – we could have tried harder. But, Helen, he started to speak. We couldn't have foreseen that, not so soon. Even if you'd never been hurt and he'd stayed at home, you couldn't have stopped him speaking, not with a cat in the house."

"No," Mum said. James decided she was studying Grandma rather like a scientist with a magnifying glass might. "I thought it was nice of Zedekiah to send him the cat, at the time. But, it was for proximity, wasn't it? The more he interacted with animals, the more likely he was to speak."

"We just wanted to keep in touch. Mr T could tell us how you were. We just wanted to know," Grandma said.

"*Right,*" Mum said. "Well, this is all spilled milk now. Even I know that. It's earlier than I ever thought, but it's also probably a good time. James is due to start at Saint Luke's in September. He's only done his year seven Induction Day so far. I'll email them when I get home and give up the place."

James almost spoke but stopped himself. Grandma had let go of the sheet and found her normal voice.

"Why would you do *that* Helen? You can't just not send him to school. The local authority will want to know where he is!"

"Actually, I can."

To James' enormous surprise, Mum chuckled a little. "I already have the paperwork and I'll look it out tomorrow. I can choose for him to attend online school."

"Really?" said Grandma. "What is that, exactly?"

"It's what it says it is - school, online. I have to pay of course, but it's Ofsted approved. I contacted the Headteacher a while ago and said I was undecided but I might want my son to enrol at some point. I was being prepared. Well, I can just call her and say that I've decided to make the jump. Then I register James as being home-schooled with the council, and that's it. It's actually incredibly simple ... You will have to go and buy him a laptop though, one he can keep with him. A small one."

"A tablet dear?"

Mum nodded. "Yes, that."

"But that's marvellous. Helen! I had no idea – about any of this. You've thought of everything."

"It's not marvellous. What will he do for friends? He'll be a loner. He won't be up on any of the stuff kids of his age know. He'll get his GCSEs, but that's all."

James blinked. He could feel a bubble of excitement rising in his middle. He wanted to jump out and tell them both not to worry. He was certain he would have plenty of friends, just not all human ones.

"Jake managed, we managed, everyone does you know." Grandma was reaching out to hold onto Mum's hand.

"Oh, I know, it's just …"

"It's OK, Helen," Grandma was smiling now. "You haven't lost him, not in any way that matters. You'll keep his respect, and he will love you so much for this. You'd only lose him if you tried to hold him back."

"And when he's older?"

"He will be old enough to make his own decisions," Grandma said. "I'll go and get them. Then Zed and I will pop and buy you a few things from the Spar for tomorrow, leave you to talk to - to *James*."

James saw Mum quickly squeezed Grandma's hand in return. Her eyes were shiny and she blinked.

"We'll take good care of him - all three of us," Grandma said.

"Four," said Mum croakily. "If you include that blasted cat."

James suddenly realised his Grandma was standing up. He nipped quietly around the bed and slipped outside, took a deep breath, then walked straight back into the ward.

"Hi Grandma!" He said. "Grandad wants to know if you and Mum want coffee?"

Artemis was cold, paw-sore, and hungry. She huddled under a wheelbarrow that was propped up behind a garden shed and tried to get herself together.

Her sense of smell was working overtime because, physically – she knew - she was in dire straits. All her senses were urging her to seek out smaller creatures she could hunt, but the wheelbarrow that provided her with some shelter from prying eyes was clouding her brain with odours of rubber, rust, metal and mould. She shivered and poked her nose out a few centimetres, whiskers taut and trembling. She breathed in slowly, allowing everything to be drawn through her olfactory nerve centres while she sifted scent from scent, thinking hard.

There was nothing out there she didn't expect: car fumes, cooking smells, vegetation, small animal life, stale scents of dog, cat, badger, fox and a fresh scent of hedgehog. Nothing unusual.

The hard pads on the bottom of Artemis' feet had become numb once more, and she flexed her claws in and out to check that all her muscles and nerve-endings were functional. Three of her claws were missing, one just starting to regrow. It threw her off-balance a tiny bit whenever she needed to grab onto a fence or branch, but she compensated well and barely noticed it now.

Artemis had been walking for four nights, including this one, and it was now nearly dawn, so she was seeking somewhere to bed down for a few hours out of harm's way. She had been travelling as fast as she could, while avoiding contact with others, and had not even allowed herself time to hunt. She gulped water on the run, from any handy vessel, but she could only go without food for so long.

Common sense began to take over and she realised that if she didn't get something to eat she would never make it to HQ anyway and all this running and hiding would have been for nothing.

Artemis stretched her neck and exposed the whole of her head. Her pupils contracted briefly in the dawn light, small black leaf shapes, before gradually expanding again to almost fill her golden irises.

Artemis was focused on everything.

The blades of grass in front of her had been recently mown and their edges looked like torn paper; they twitched individually as if little electrical currents ran through them. Artemis registered each movement and knew if it was a worm pulling at the roots, a vole scrabbling across the lawn, an insect bumbling through the stems.

The same for the crackling tree trunk, alive with tiny insect life waking to the new day, the fluttering leaves snapping against the apple tree, the thrumming wings of night-time creatures heading for nooks and crannies in which to spend the daylight hours.

Artemis plotted the course of the garden fence and felt it beneath her feet even before she had moved, imagining how many seconds it would take to traverse and reach the garden next-door. Her ears twitched, delicate little heartbeats, as she counted down the sound of hedgehog bristles pinging off the wooden slats while the creature bumbled along the other side of the fence in search of bugs for breakfast. The sounds grew fainter with its progress, then moved direction at the corner, where the fence met a wall. She had measured the distance from the sounds and heard the tiny scrape of bristle on brick before the creature wandered out across the grass once more.

Without even scaling the fence, Artemis had pictured the terrain beyond. She judged that she could move on without danger of discovery, to find a wilder garden in which to hunt for food, or a patch of waste ground for preference.

In a flash, she was out from the barrow and over the fence, sheltered behind the tree and listening intently to the sounds of the garden further ahead.

Seconds later she was over the wall.

By the time the sun rose properly, Artemis was crouched inside a broken, upturned plastic crate, half buried in the long grass beside a canal. She was crunching hungrily on the carcass of a vole, her nose already wrinkling as she caught the scent of a mouse trail running up the bank.

She swallowed hurriedly and tiptoed rapidly after the scent, glancing upwards every few seconds, using the long grass to shield her from sight.

"What's up, hrrr?" Mr T queried padding into Ops from the living room.

"Ah, T... Missed check-in," said Agent Zed, seated at the Ops computer. A red bar onscreen was flashing white capital letters: ALERT. A message beneath it read: *Checkpoint Missed - 01:01:00.* The message blinked off and returned, to read: *01:01:01.*" It continued second by second to chart the absence.

"Em!" Zed yelled, making Mr T's hairs stand on end briefly.

"They're out," Mr T said. "Taking Helen home, remember? Hrrr. It may be nothing you know," though his tail twitched, once. "Who is it?"

"Artemis." Zed said. "You coming?"

Mr T was already heading back through the living room.

"Hurry up, Zed," he threw over his shoulder, waiting by the front door.

Agent Zed had an EagleView GPS Device attached to the handlebars of the bike he now wheeled carefully out of the garage. Mr T watched him click on the dot that corresponded to Artemis and considered the information the dot gave them. She was about 15 miles away and headed in a straight line - towards HQ, as far as they could see. The problem was that she hadn't communicated with anyone in a week. All operatives who were chipped could be tracked. Mr T was also chipped and so knew, just as well as Agent Zed, that when those chips came within three metres of each other EagleView automatically reset both. If an EagleView chip had not reset for a week, an alarm was generated on the system. It was a failsafe device, to make sure the agents were all OK. Generally, agents needed to communicate all the time, unless there was a particular reason not to: undercover, for instance.

"She's not been undercover, T." Agent Zed seemed to be reading his thoughts. So Artemis was either avoiding, or being kept from, contact with other agents. "She's heading straight for HQ, I'm sure of it. So she can't have been taken. I don't think this is Misant work –" Zed was thinking aloud.

"But then," said Mr T, "she's clearly staying deliberately out of touch, so *something's* wrong." He trailed off, trying hard to think of a reason for the alert that was not related to Misants.

As an answer, Agent Zed bent down and hauled Mr T into the air, before dumping him inelegantly into the carrier on the back of the bike. Jamming the helmet down on his head, he tapped his pockets, hopped onto the seat and set off.

Mr T curled into a ball and weathered the bumps in the road. One thing you could say for a Harley, they had good suspension. It was a big bike and the carrier was roomy: padded, but with custom-made air holes and small windows in three sides. There were worse ways to travel.

Mr T reminded himself that agents had gone off the communications grid before. Some suffered burn-out and just wanted to be left alone. There was one memorable occasion when a Lurcher in Dorset had become locked in a freight car. The operative who eventually found him reported that he was only alive because part of the cargo had been boxes of UHT milk. Mr T's train of thought did not stop, however. Sometimes an agent who had lost contact was found no longer alive. A stationary dot could mean the worst. Mr T was cheered by the fact that Artemis was clearly on the move. Through the windows, he watched the houses fall away as they left the suburbs, and the landscape gradually became greener, the air fresher.

After a while the bright colours of a narrow-boat, painted with red and orange roses, flashed past and Mr T registered the babbling noise of water distinct from the rushing noise of air, carrying with it the mixed scents of mud and weeds. The Harley reared up over a small bridge and, from his vantage point, Mr T could see swirling green, brown and white water churning into a lock a short way along the canal below.

The bike stopped and Agent Zed turned around to speak.

"I don't get it, T," he called. "She's stopped moving. She ought to be around here somewhere, we ought to be able to see her."

Zed hauled Mr T out again and placed him on the wall of the bridge, from where they both scanned the canal and its banks. Mr T jumped down and they walked slowly towards the lock gate, turning their heads left and right, Mr T narrowing his eyelids as he sifted the various smells and sounds in his head. Zed leaned on the gatepost and studied the GPS which he had detached from the bike. He frowned, saying:

"What –?"

"*What?*" echoed Mr T.

"It's reset. Artemis' EagleView chip reset. We should be right on top of her. Where on Earth … ?"

Zed's voice trailed off, as he turned around and peered down into the murky water of the lock, which was beginning to settle. Mr T followed Zed's gaze, feeling the fur along his back beginning to rise up hair by hair.

CHAPTER 13

VARIOUS TRAVELLERS

EVIE HAD BEEN instructed by Loulou that they could only take the train as far as Godalming, as their destination was secret. They had therefore taken the bus from the train station as far as a village by the name of Peaslake. Then they walked, for miles. After a couple of hours they found the River Tillingbourne and followed it to Acton Worthy – more of a hamlet than a village, isolated and quiet.

Evie ran her tongue over her dry lips as Loulou took several long drinks from the river itself. She had drained her bottle of water back at Peaslake. Loulou, unsuccessfully, urged Evie to lean over the bank and take a drink alongside her.

"You are going to have to get over all this if you're working in the field," Loulou said.

"I am *not* drinking un-boiled river water!" Evie replied, annoyed because she was tired and thirsty. "It might be OK for you, but I'd probably get dysentery or something and end up dead. That's not going to be a lot of help to you 'out in the field' is it?"

"A little dramatic." said Loulou. "If you insist on being quite so precious, then you'd better remember to pack enough water next time. The problem with *human* operatives is their intolerance."

Evie stared down at Loulou and said, through gritted teeth:

"Yes, *our* intolerance. *That's* the problem."

By that time, they had crossed a field and come to a stile which was part of an overgrown garden fence. Evie clambered over it while Loulou shoved her whole bulk through the gap and, amazingly, emerged on the other side. There was a gravel path, broken up by weeds which took them around the corner of a house in the direction of a dark green front door. The paintwork was a little chipped and seemed not to have been refreshed for a good few years.

"We're here," Loulou announced. Evie looked around in all directions, saw nothing but the run-down house and garden, and turned back towards Loulou who was waiting patiently at the door.

"*Really?*" Evie said. "This is HQ?"

Loulou sighed.

"Lesson number, I have no idea, look beyond the obvious. Don't assume the HQ of a secret organisation will have a shiny big sign and a flag outside. Will you knock?"

Evie, feeling somewhat flushed, did as she was asked.

There was a barely audible electronic whirring sound and the light caught a tiny black lense in a corner of the porch as it adjusted to focus on the callers. Evie heard a quiet click and Loulou woofed:

"In we go!"

She pushed the door, and it swung inwards, silently.

Artemis had followed the trail of the mouse for several feet before it just disappeared. The strong rodent scent was replaced by a whiff of something else that drifted away almost before Artemis could place it: sparrowhawk. Artemis sighed. The mouse had been taken by someone else. She would have to find another food source or travel on managing with what she'd had.

Time was a factor. The longer she was out in the open the more chance of being intercepted but, the hungrier she was, the slower she would be. Artemis struggled to decide what was for the best and resolved to go back down near the canal to see if she could find a luckless water vole or even a frog or worm and, if not, then keep going at least for a few hours before stopping again.

She glanced nervously at the sky, which was clear, scented the air then crept out from a clump of weeds to head back down the bank. The moment she did so, she heard a high-pitched scream from overhead and registered a grey, white and reddish blur descending towards her like a stone. Artemis's heart seemed to bounce inside her chest as she ran like a streak towards the water and along its edge. There was a bridge up ahead and she sprinted for it with the little energy she had left.

The scream had been a call: *She's here! She's here!*

The high-pitched note carried for miles and Artemis knew exactly what would happen next: soon the sparrowhawk would have company and he was clearly no friend to her. Artemis's fur stuck out as if she had been electrified and her eyes, pale moons of fear, scanned the surroundings as she ran for any nook of shelter or safety.

Being hidden from the sky was her first priority and she almost fell over herself as she hit the ground under the bridge, sensing the updraft of air as the sparrowhawk stopped short, then went over the top instead.

Artemis knew that in a straight fight a sparrowhawk was too small to do her serious damage but – as she crouched against the bridge wall, shivering and sucking air in and out – she heard the hoarse, metallic call of a Harris hawk: *We see you!*

Artemis was desperate. She knew all about Harris hawks' unusual way of hunting: in packs known as 'casts'. Artemis was well aware that she had no hope of defending herself against more than one hawk. The sparrowhawk had gone, his job done, and it would only be a matter of moments before the Harris hawks drove Artemis out from under the bridge. They would fly at her one after another and she would become weaker with every strike. Artemis could see the lock, just a few yards away. A narrowboat had been through a moment ago, cheerfully painted, with its human occupants oblivious to Artemis who had been just a few feet away from them.

Now Artemis raced for her life, towards the arm of the lock, and she did not look up. There was a small gap beneath the arm, where it met the gate itself. It was not very wide, and she had no idea if she could crouch small enough inside to fully avoid prying beaks and talons, but there was no other shelter and she had no more time to think.

She slid to a halt underneath the arm, skittering perilously close to the brick edge of the lock itself and glimpsing the churning water below. As she did, yet another claw snagged and was pulled free. Artemis teetered on the brink of the wall, scrabbling with her back feet, sensing a rush of air as wings beat downwards above her.

Just a short distance away, Finley, a springer spaniel standing on the stern of the brightly coloured narrowboat, caused his owners great consternation as – for no apparent reason – he suddenly and uncharacteristically leapt from his station and landed in the murky green water of the canal, with an enormous splash.

He then paddled like crazy, seeming panicked, yet heading – not back towards the boat – but for the safety of dry land. His owners called to each other, and the slow-moving canal boat began to head for the shore also, where they took some moments securing it before being able to disembark and follow their pet.

Hauling himself out of the canal was an effort fuelled by adrenalin, as it was not something Finley would normally have attempted. Springer spaniels are not as athletic as the name might suggest, having fairly short legs relative to their body mass. But they are determined, strong and have good hearts that can carry them forward against adversity. Finley scrabbled up the bank, cold, sodden and muddy. Then he charged - a bundle of dog-shaped fury - back under the bridge and towards the lock where three large, reddish-brown birds were diving in turn at the wooden lock arm, scraping it with their talons and screaming to each other.

Finley could not understand what they were saying but he had seen the skinny grey cat that shot along the canal bank and he knew that, even for Harris hawks, this was unusual behaviour - in broad daylight, near people, and all over a cat. Finley just felt deep down inside that something was very wrong with what he was seeing.

He tore into the birds, barking for all he was worth, growling at them and jumping to meet them as they tried to strike him. He shouted out between barks:

"Are you there? Are you alright?"

But there was no response.

As he had known they would, Finley's owners now caught up to him. They were deeply shocked, and shouted at the birds as they ran up, waving their arms. The birds took another half-hearted swoop before rising upwards and taking off east, in formation, becoming mere dots in the sky within seconds.

"Oh, my *goodness!*" The woman called out. "Finley! What on Earth do you think you're doing?"

The man bent down and patted Finley's head whilst, confusingly, saying:

"Bad boy! You leave those birds alone!"

The birds, of course, were now long gone and the man was clearly relieved that Finley appeared unharmed.

"Oh my Lord, you are *filthy*," the woman carried on. "Come on, back to the boat. Geoff, you'll have to *scrub* him. We'd better get moored up properly."

The dog and people receded along the bank, though Finley seemed oddly reluctant to go with them and they had to cajole him.

"Thank you," came a very shaky, small voice from the vicinity of the lock.

"Will you be OK?" Finley barked.

"Are you an agent?" the voice asked in return.

"Agent? No. Are you?"

"Finley, be quiet," the man said sternly. "They've gone now. Come on boy."

"Thank you so much. I'll be fine."

Finley very much hoped she was right.

Artemis was actually far from fine, but she didn't want her brave rescuer to worry. If he wasn't an agent, he was surely pro-Lifelink. There was nothing else he could do now, and Artemis was extremely grateful for the dog's quick thinking. She reflected for a second on the fact that good people were everywhere. And for the sake of all those good people, she needed to go on, right now.

She extended her right foreleg tentatively, but a sharp pain shot up through her shoulder and into her neck. She gasped, and flopped back down, her chest heaving as she tried to get her breath back.

Artemis realised abruptly that she was in a very bad way. She felt a rising wave of panic that was not helped by the harsh sound of traffic on the road overhead, louder and louder … until Artemis just stopped hearing it. Her translucent third eyelids closed, her dulled irises rolling upwards, until both eyes shut completely. Her body finally ceased trembling and was still.

Two of the Harris hawks that had attacked Artemis peeled away from the third and alighted on trees, a quarter of a mile apart from each other, taking up watch. The third called out, a harsh squawk, and wheeled herself around to face North-West. Her muscular wings beat down on the updraft of warm air, once, twice, then faster - until she was flying steadily in a straight line, barely slower than the cars that were far below. Realistically, she could not maintain her speed the whole way. It would take her at least half a day – given she would have to stop to hunt – but, even allowing for that, she should be there long before nightfall. The message was hers to take, and swiftly.

CHAPTER 14

A NARROW ESCAPE

ARTEMIS WAS BEING dragged back towards the land of the living by a dull, red light but she resisted its pull and drifted off towards the darkness. As she did so, however, a sharp pain at the back of her head threw her abruptly into reality and she gasped. The sound came out as a plaintive mewing.

"Hi," whispered a human voice. She focussed on the outline of a boy standing beside her, who reached out and gently stroked the ridges of her backbone, his eyes full of concern. "Don't worry," he said. "You're safe now. I'm just going to go and fetch someone. I'll be right back … Grandma!" Artemis heard the voice from further away. "She's awake!"

"Oh excellent. I'm just coming." A different voice, still human.

Artemis had no idea where she was.

"Where am I?" she whispered.

The boy had returned, but a much older human leaned forward from behind him and observed Artemis through simply enormous, warm brown eyes. No, through … *Glasses* – Artemis fished the word from deep down inside her foggy brain.

"Artemis, isn't it? My name is Agent Em. You are in a secret Ops room run by Lifelink South. You were quite badly injured. You have been sedated, and we had to perform a small operation, but you'll be fine in a few days."

"A few *days!*" Artemis was wide awake now. She jerked her head up as she spoke, then dropped it down again speedily. "Oh! *Oww*, my head!"

The old human nodded. "Yes, I'm sorry, you'll probably feel a bit the worse for wear."

"But you don't *understand*," Artemis tried again to sit up. "I *have* to get to HQ. As soon as possible. I can't wait a few days – you'll have to get me there."

The woman made little shaking movements with her head and breathed out through her nose. "Artemis, I can't. You're not going anywhere for a while. Your leg was hurt, and the bone was very badly broken. I'm afraid I had to replace it. You can't even start physio until tomorrow."

A chill crept along Artemis's spine. "How long have I been sedated?"

"About a day and a half now. It's Thursday afternoon. Why?"

"Oh – no. You have transport don't you? You'll have to go instead. You have to take a message."

"I can email them, dear," said the old lady. "I can send it today."

"Is it safe? It has to go to Agent Singh and no-one else. Is it secure?"

The woman frowned, placing her hands on her hips. "Well, it should be. We encrypt our emails."

"So, it couldn't be intercepted, by Misant operatives?"

"No, I don't think so. No – it couldn't."

Artemis allowed her muscles to relax, to feel less like coiled springs.

"OK – can we do it now?" she purred.

"I'll just get Agent Zed." The old lady left, but the boy stayed to keep watch.

Evie followed Agent Loulou through a dowdy hallway and into the kitchen of the house, that appeared not to have been updated in the last fifty years. There was no-one around.

"Through here." Loulou lifted her paw and tapped at a knot in the wooden jamb of a door leading off the kitchen, presumably to an old-fashioned pantry. The door swung open outwards and Loulou hurried through. Evie stuck with her and the door closed itself behind them. A light clicked on as it did so, revealing a small rectangular room with a descending staircase opposite them.

"A cellar?" Evie said. She registered a distant humming, perhaps of machinery, rising upwards. Loulou did not respond, but began bumping clumsily down the stairs ahead, with Evie hurrying to follow. At the bottom, Loulou turned through an archway which exited unexpectedly into a huge, brightly-lit room full of busy people – human and animal. Evie stood, stock still. It was a few moments before she realised her bottom lip had dropped and her mouth was literally hanging open. She promptly clamped it shut. No-one was watching, however - except Loulou, who was standing a few feet away with her head turned to look back.

"Are you coming?"

Evie hurriedly caught up, following Loulou between lines of workstations, with maybe fifty humans engrossed in computer screens or talking on the phone. Next to many of the desks, and *on* many of the desks, were feathered and furred operatives deep in earnest conversation. The hum she had heard had been people, going about their work. Along one wall there was a massive screen that was split into sections showing different views of maps, lists of names, photos of people of various species - too much information for Evie to make sense of as she marched past. Everything was very bright and clean.

At the end of the room was another, smaller office, separated off by a glass panel through which Evie could see a man standing beside a desk and talking energetically on the phone. This office seemed to be Loulou's destination.

The man looked like a cross between an Army Major and the Prime Minister - not tall, but definitely in command, with a dark suit, blue tie and short, sharply-cut hair. Evie became conscious of a great desire to turn around and run, back to Kath or even Matron – anywhere really – rather than be here where she felt so utterly out of place.

She abruptly registered the warm, furry flank of Loulou brushing against her legs, comforting and familiar, as her tutor dropped back a little to walk in step. The man in the glass office replaced the phone, and beckoned Loulou and Evie into the room. Loulou pushed open the door and Evie slipped in behind her, but stopped just inside, as Loulou headed towards the large, shiny, metal and wood desk.

"*Agent*," the man boomed. "Excellent to see you again. It's been *far* too long. You're looking well. The teaching role must be suiting you! But not so much that you don't want to be back out in the field, I understand?"

Loulou sat on her haunches and waited patiently, clearly both at ease in her surroundings and very familiar with listening to – her boss?

"And *you*, young lady." The man adjusted his gaze to focus on Evie. "Come up here, we don't bite!" He chuckled. "Well I don't at least! You must be The Amazing Evie? Destined to be an asset, I am *reliably* informed. *Sai Singh* - call me Singh!" Evie shuffled a few steps nearer to the desk but remained silent as no words formed in her head. She smiled, to show willing. "Mm, HQ can be a bit much at first glance. Here –" Singh gestured towards a couple of low-slung chairs beside a small table and stepped out from behind his desk. "Take a seat."

Evie obliged by perching on the edge of the nearest chair and Loulou ambled over to make a third point in their conversational triangle.

"Now, *Lou*," Agent Singh began, and Evie had to stifle a giggle.

Loulou glanced over at her sternly. Agent Singh paused, then looked past the pair towards the offices outside. He still addressed Loulou.

"You know, Lou, Evie has yet to meet some of our other redoubtable friends. Agents Bouncer and Poppet for instance. Or perhaps Agent *Puddles* over there." His mouth twitched at the corners. Evie stared through the glass to where, on the edge of a nearby desk, sat a black-and-white Tom. He was indicating something onscreen by gesturing with his nose, while a human operative clicked a computer mouse. Evie had swallowed hard at the words 'Agent Puddles,' and felt her cheeks flush with the effort. Agent Singh, however, was grinning widely.

"Probationary Agent Evie," he said. "Your best asset over the next few years will be a well-developed sense of humour, I assure you. That is a quality that can be in short supply in times of strife. I urge you to hold onto it. Or - I should say - let it loose, rather."

Evie allowed a small, undignified snort of laughter to burst out.

"Agent *Lou ... lou* and I are old friends, Evie – we don't stand on ceremony these days," Singh said. "I called you here initially, Lou, to send you on a routine scouting run. I thought it might be a good way to ease you back into the field and show our newest member the ropes. But, I have just received a rather disturbing message from Ops South so, instead, I need to drop you back in at the deep end as it were. I hope you'll be OK with that?"

He waited for Loulou to respond and Evie saw the corner of Loulou's mouth curl upwards as she observed Agent Singh, her head tilted to one side. Evie edged backwards in her seat.

"*Well*, thank Heaven for Ops South then! *Scouting* run? No wonder you didn't give me any details *before* I got here. Yes, I will be '*OK*' with a mission, Singh – and I'd be grateful if you didn't consider me for anything else in future."

"Point taken." Singh grinned. Then his face set into harder lines. "I believe you both know Agent Artemis?" Evie was all ears at the mention of the familiar name and studied Singh's face as he talked. "I had an encrypted email from Ops South. Artemis is with Agents Em and Zed currently. She is, by all accounts, injured – quite severely. Injuries she acquired during a journey back from her last mission which, I'm afraid, failed – no fault of hers I might add." Evie sat up straight, ready to quiz Agent Singh for the details – but she need not have worried as he leaned forward, arms braced, and began retelling the story.

"It was a fairly standard thing - young boy with a recessive speaker gene. Family canine, known Lifelink supporter - a German Shepherd," he added this last with a nod towards Loulou, who huffed slightly in return. "Artemis arrived on the scene, but the boy had vanished. She says she hung around for a couple of days, parents in and out of the house, dog the same, but no sign of the boy. So, she waited until the dog was outside alone, took up safe vantage – garage roof I believe – and tried to make contact. The dog not only didn't *speak*, he tried to *attack* her – somewhat pointlessly of course. Anyway, she remained in the vicinity for another day - and the boy came home."

Agent Singh had begun pacing up and down the length of his office. Evie watched Loulou's head turning this way and that as she followed Singh's movements like a spectator at a tennis match.

"The dog wouldn't let her anywhere near the house, but in the afternoon when the boy was out in the garden alone, she saw her chance and went right up to the lad to speak. Didn't know when she'd get another opportunity. But he didn't understand a word, not a word. Shoo-ed her away if you please. She waited till the dog was let out again, but it was as if they were both non-speakers. Artemis knew the German Shepherd at least was lying, so she hung around until she could get him alone."

"And did she?" Loulou said. Evie could understand her impatience.

Agent Singh checked his pacing but, full of energy, now began gesturing widely with his arms.

"She did. Artemis said – apparently – he could bark 'all he liked' but the humans would only take him inside and she'd stay exactly where she was till he came back out. Climbed down to the fence and demanded that he answer her – which, in the end, he did. He *said:* 'I can't. They're watching. Please just go away.' Of course, she didn't – she wanted to know *who* was watching. By this time, the dog was scratching at the door and whining to be let in - German Shepherd, prime of his life, terrified of a *tabby!*" Singh rolled his eyes. "So, Artemis tried a different tack and asked why the boy wouldn't speak and he said: 'Can't. Pills. *Now* will you leave me alone?' And that's all she got because the humans took him inside and he didn't come back out. By then she'd been there over three days, for a lost cause, so she decided to report back."

Singh took a breath, rubbing his hand over his forehead.

"Agent Loulou, have you met Agent Newman? Just outside Windsor? Human operative."

"Oh! Yes – I have … once – well, not met exactly. He was at a briefing we had on Misant activity in the South. Must be a couple of years ago now. Quiet type, not sure I took to him. Why?"

"You have good instincts, Lou," said Singh. "Agent Artemis quite rightly assumed she should make contact and share the intel asap. Agent Newman was the closest operative, so that's where she headed. Except he found her first." Singh folded his arms and sat on the edge of his desk. "Approached her out of nowhere, just walking along the road. She's a sensible operative, was keeping to the hedgerows, when suddenly Agent Newman's head leans over a gate and says: 'Agent Artemis? They told me I'd find you here.' She of course assumed 'they' meant someone from Lifelink, got in his car and went back to his base."

Singh jumped back up and resumed pacing.

"When they got into the house, Agent Newman – just Newman from now on, actually – said 'I'll leave you to speak to the boss,' showed her into the conservatory and left. Artemis turns around and she's face-to-face with a badger! Right there in broad daylight, in Newman's house!"

"The *boss?*" Loulou echoed.

"Exactly." Singh sighed. "And speaking. Long story short, this badger – name of Titan – was a Misant leader! Artemis was given a choice - join the Misants or suffer the consequences. She's hardly any match for a badger, especially one she's shut inside a room with."

"So? She …?" Evie said.

"She's no fool, Evie. She opted to join the Misants."

"*What?*"

People on the other side of the thick glass partition raised their heads and Evie felt her face colouring again. Loulou remained quiet until Singh – who was now holding up his index finger at them - carried on.

"This Titan spent a good few hours talking with her – threatening her - but she managed to convince him she was genuinely willing to defect. I gather he then ordered Newman to have Artemis 'disinfected', which turned out to be a euphemism for a small operation to remove the EagleView chip. Anyway, Newman went to make a phone call, and left her with this Doberman."

Singh stopped walking and sat back on the low chair, though he was tapping his fingers on the arm.

"The doorbell rang, and the Doberman took his eye off Artemis to look through the window, and she ran straight for the stairs! He went after her of course, and I can only imagine what he would have done, but she got through an upstairs window. Fell – but you know cats – and just fled." Singh paused and shook his head.

"So she got away and – what?" Loulou growled. "Walked back to Ops South?"

"More or less," said Singh. "It's clear that the Misants have an active air presence. And the fact that a man who we thought was a Lifelink agent is now one of them – well, we hardly know who we can trust any more." Singh was leaning forwards now. "Neither did Artemis, which is why she was headed straight here. She only made it to Ops South, and she'll be in recuperation for a while yet. Damned brave stuff. It's this Titan character we're interested in. We've never been able to identify, much less name, a Misant leader before. Usually they're kept well hidden. Wasn't local either – he'd been brought in to check on the troops. That's bad news, if *badgers* are willing to depart from home turf … What do *they* know that we don't? They're either confident or desperate - we *need* intel."

"Sorry," Evie cut in. "This Newman guy –" Singh gestured for her to continue. "If he's a double agent, can't you track him?"

"Good point, Evie. You've hit the nail on the head: EagleView … We thought we *were* tracking him. When Agent Artemis told her story, we did exactly that – followed the signal to the agent – except it wasn't. It led us to a house a few streets away from Newman's base. The signal was coming from a Burmese cat, non-speaker."

Singh turned the palms of his hands upwards and shrugged.

"The only explanation is that Newman's chip had been deliberately removed and implanted elsewhere. His base had a For Sale sign outside and we're guessing he hadn't been there for some time. No idea where the house was he took Agent Artemis - nor how long he's been a Misant. I've got operatives going back through the files to see if his EagleView chip registered at the group briefings. We know *he* was there so, if his signal wasn't, we'll know he was already operating against us. Until we have that, we have no idea how much information might have been passed on."

"And the real problem," Loulou said, "Is that if we had one leak, we probably have a few more, right?"

Singh nodded.

"As ever, Agent Loulou."

Loulou dropped her chin onto her paws. Evie smiled at the thought that Loulou had clearly put her head in her hands to think. She waited, watching the two senior agents but, after a while, she coughed politely.

Singh looked up.

"Agent Singh … sir," Evie ventured. "You said Loulou and I could help?"

"I did," Singh agreed. "You can get a good night's sleep then go tomorrow. I'll let them know. I need you to talk to Artemis - and *then* I want you to track down this Titan creature and see if you can't find out what he's planning. I don't need to add, but for your benefit Evie I *shall*, that it's neither an easy nor a particularly *safe* mission. Agent Loulou is one of our best." Loulou 'hrmphed' modestly. "And she has some good contacts – well, hopefully … but, there's something else, some*one* else I need you to check out. It could be important, especially now we're on heightened alert…"

Evie saw Loulou's stance tighten at Singh's words.

"Agent Jake," Singh said.

Loulou stood up: "You haven't *found* him?"

"No, no - sorry. It's not that. He was a great loss. I wish we *had* found him – but that trail is long cold. He had a son, though, a boy called James. He's only eleven, but he's just started to speak."

Evie reflected on how odd that sentence would sound to anyone who didn't understand.

"Is that very young?" she said.

"It is," agreed Singh. "Unusually young. His father, though, had started to speak before he was ten - and I am wondering ..."

Loulou had begun pacing up and down the room, but she stopped and regarded Singh intently.

"You think he may have the same talent?"

"Exactly."

"And I assume he is with Agents Em and Zed?"

"He is."

"OK then," said Loulou.

"OK then," confirmed Singh.

Loulou headed towards the door and Evie jumped up to follow her. Singh returned to his desk, pressed a button on the phone and angled his chair towards the screen in front of him - immediately lost in the next task, fingers tapping the keyboard. Evie's mouth twitched into a brief smile, as she hurried out after Loulou, wondering if she should have said goodbye.

"Loulou," Evie stage-whispered, as they wound their way through the noisy workplace. "What *talent?*"

CHAPTER 15

HEALING
AND DESTROYING

ONCE ARTEMIS WAS confident her information had been passed successfully to Agent Singh, she relaxed a great deal, which Agent Em said was the very best thing for her as she would heal much faster that way.

Artemis had begun physio and was walking tentatively for a few minutes in the morning and afternoon, with James supporting her by holding her midriff as she took her first, somewhat shaky steps.

"The indignity!" Artemis complained. "Being carried around by a child."

"Oh, be quiet," Mr T said, "and concentrate on moving that leg *properly*."

"He has a point," said Em. "Because, as I was saying, I had to replace the bone. The leg is greatly prosthetic now. I have implanted generated muscle and nerve tissue but retained your own skin."

"Ugh," spat Artemis.

"I don't take it you'd rather lose the leg, hrrr?" Mr T stretched his own legs, arching his back. Artemis gave him a long, hard look.

"Yes, thank you Agent," Em said. "Anyway, I also took the liberty of attaching two percent carbon steel claws, so they'll work a bit better than the ones nature gave you. And you won't lose them, not unless you lose the leg," she added with a grin. "James, pop her down over there will you. We'll rest for a bit."

"We?" queried Artemis, but no-one responded.

"Basically," Em said, "Everything prosthetic attaches to your own tissue. You need to use it as much as possible to get the messages travelling back and forth. The more you use it, the stronger it will get."

"I'm sure," Artemis sighed. "But it doesn't feel like *my* leg. I don't know how to describe it. I mean, I can feel my leg – the old leg – but then when I walk it's like … It's a bit like I have three front legs! The one that was fine, the one my brain expects to be there, and then this other leg that moves of its own accord when I walk with the old one!"

"Weird," muttered Mr T.

"It is," said Artemis.

"I meant *you* ... You think you have *three* front legs!"

Em ignored them and carried on talking.

"You have phantom limb syndrome. It'll fade. Gradually you'll just get used to the new one, trust me. You need to keep walking – with all your legs – and you'll soon see I'm telling the truth."

Artemis took a deep breath. *Humans* - they were both useful and intensely irritating! She regarded Mr T through narrowed eyelids, conceding that the same could also be said of some cats.

The tall man with grey-and-rust coloured hair, prominent brows and a rough, stubbled face, felt a crawling sensation as the small hairs on his neck and shoulders nudged his nerves, making him shiver, suddenly.

He had been leaning with his hands on his knees staring at nothing, lost in a train of thought that furrowed his brow and turned the corners of his mouth grimly downwards. Now though, he raised himself up, from the massive, fallen tree trunk that lay across the pitted floor of the copse, its giant, upturned roots sheltering a thousand tiny creatures.

He turned around, just in time to see a red-brown missile crash through the tiny leaves at the top of a silver birch and plummet like a stone to the ground beside him. The landing was clumsy and the large bird rolled sideways, it strong yellow talons grappling with the turf to find a hold.

The man seemed unsurprised, however, and stood by waiting for the Harris hawk to remain upright and still. The bird found its balance, then fluttered up onto the end of the fallen tree where the bark was scorched black, and preened its wing feathers a little, before it tried to speak.

"Stranger," it croaked, lowering its head respectfully. "I am exhausted, forgive me, but I need to speak to you." The man inclined his head and the hawk continued. "There is a Lifelink agent who has returned to Singh, who knows we have infiltrated their organisation."

The man remained silent and watched the hawk, his face displaying an expression of curious detachment as he observed the creature, distantly.

He raised the corner of one eyebrow minimally and the hawk continued.

"The agent who lied to us, then escaped. The operatives who allowed it have been punished, of course, but we could not recapture her. I –" the hawk paused, unsure of herself. "I could not recapture her."

As the hawk had been talking the sun had crept lower in the sky, and the world was gradually being sapped of its colour, as dusk fell, painting everything around them in blues and greys. A chill breeze lifted the hawk's chest feathers and she shook herself to realign them.

The man they called Stranger stared at the Harris hawk, considering. Then he looked away and focussed for a moment on a gap at the edge of the copse. The shadows there broke apart, to resolve themselves into a black-and-white snout that belonged to the lumbering form of a huge, male badger. Seeing it, the hawk immediately flapped down from the tree trunk and mantled her wings, head lowered, as if bowing. In response, however, the badger rushed towards her, snarling, then fastened his jaws onto the skin beneath her auburn plumage and shook her – like a dog with a toy, growling. His task done, he turned back towards the trees, stamping carelessly over an outstretched wing as he left.

The man gazed for a while at the limp form of the hawk, bloodied and dirty in the grass, then nodded once – as if satisfied – before sauntering off to follow the badger. The two forms slipped between the trees and strode across the fields beyond - figures fading from sight as they dissolved into twilight.

The Harris hawk's eyes were glazed now, and she was almost completely still, but for an increasingly shallow movement of feathers on her chest. The clearing was empty and silent. The sky beyond the copse had darkened to navy, tree trunks running down it like lines of nothing. Small sounds rustled on the cooling air; a few last shadows flitted between the branches.

After a while, a larger, darker shape emerged from the gloom and made its way over to the fallen hawk.

CHAPTER 16

NEW DISCOVERIES

O N THE BUS to Ops South (otherwise known as 45 Cromwell Street) Evie found it highly amusing that Loulou allowed the two children, on the seat in front, to ruffle her fur and call her a 'good dog,' as their Dad watched approvingly.

Evie, as they disembarked, told Loulou that she was "a very good dog, a very good dog indeed, yes she was!"

Loulou reminded Evie that although this was, of course, generally true - like all dogs she also had the ability to bite those people who upset her. Evie fell silent, feeling a wide grin stretching her check muscles, and blinking to hide the twinkle in her eyes.

James stumbled down the stairs on Friday morning, yawning widely. He had stayed up late on Thursday, helping Grandma perform an operation. Like the black cat before, this stray dog had turned out to be a non-speaker who had been hit by a passing car, the driver of which had driven on regardless. Grandma had had to operate immediately, as the little mutt had lost a lot of blood, but when she checked him over she had discovered he was chipped. They didn't know how this family pet had managed to escape his home and get lost but, as James found out, Grandad had access to the online pet registry system - 'a little thing your Dad set up for us.' Grandad soon found out where the dog's home was. The plan was to quietly deliver him back to where he came from after he had had a few hours to recover. The owners would never know what had happened.

His head full of the little dog's rescue, James padded into the kitchen and made himself a rather full bowl of Frosted Squares, which he carried carefully back to the living room. He plonked himself down in one of the armchairs and reached for the remote.

There was a cough.

"Er, hi," said a voice from the sofa.

James started, and whipped his head round, slopping a spoonful of milk onto his pyjamas as he did so. On the sofa sat a young woman. She was wearing red woolly socks and ripped jeans, sitting cross-legged, sipping a mug of coffee. Her hair was stuffed under a black baseball cap and her T-shirt depicted an angry young woman with the words JOIN THE RESISTANCE.

"Oh, sorry," she said. "I thought I'd better say something."

James gathered himself together and fished around in his brain for a suitable expression, while saying:

"No, that's OK. Sorry – I'm a bit sleepy still I guess," he laughed awkwardly, felt awkward, and continued: "So, you're -?"

"Evie," she said.

"Ah. Er, do you know my Grandparents then?" James asked.

He was doing his best at polite conversation, which he assumed was what the situation required.

"No," Evie said.

James was struggling. Why was there a rather rough-looking girl, sitting on Grandma's sofa, who didn't know them? Just as he tried to form a sensible question, the door to Ops swung open - and a very large dog padded into the room. It was nothing like the little mongrel from the operation.

James put down his cereal on the bookcase and rubbed his eyes.

"Is the dog yours?"

The woman called Evie spluttered a little through her coffee, swallowed hard, and grinned at the dog.

"Hardly," said the dog. "I assume you are James?"

"Oh." James felt that life was being really unfair, tricking him with all this before he was properly awake. Considering where he was and what he knew, he should obviously have expected to be addressed by the canine in the room – but he was tired and unfocussed, and had been up half the night assisting with a perfectly ordinary dog. Besides which, he was used to cats.

The room fell silent while the dog and Evie exchanged a glance, which James felt was probably about him. Just then, Grandad – thank goodness – came striding in from the hallway with a big smile on his face.

"All done!" He said, loudly. "Safely back with his owners: successful covert ops!" Grandad chuckled. James realised he meant the little mongrel.

"Oh!" James said. "Already? I thought we were keeping him for a day?"

"Your Grandma decided he was doing exceptionally well, so we sent him back. Sooner the better. His owners were very glad to see him too. I watched from over the road. I think they'll be keeping a better eye on him in future!" Grandad sounded very pleased with himself. He turned to address the visitors. "And I see you've met young Jim? Er, James? If the pleasantries are over we should probably get down to business. James shall you pop up and get dressed, lad, and I'll be in Ops with our guests?"

James was tempted to say that he hadn't had any breakfast yet, but curiosity over the guests won out, and he hurried to dump his cereal bowl in the sink as the other three headed into the study.

As they followed the old guy through to the next room Evie was deciding to herself that, if that was the wonder child they had just met, she for one was unimpressed. Her mouth twitched into a smirk as she remembered his comment about Loulou. Some speaker James was.

"You'll be wanting a debrief with Artemis," Agent Zed suggested. "Em says she's up to it so, now we're all here, we can get going."

"Don't you want to wait for the boy?" Loulou asked.

"Do you think we should?" Agent Zed said. "As a sort of lesson, is that what you're thinking?"

"Yes, and it might be useful."

Evie knew Loulou had trained several new members of Lifelink, because they had discussed it on the way. Apparently, Loulou's grandfather had been Probationary Agent Jake's tutor many years previously. Loulou was very proud that her family line went back in the history of Lifelink for many generations. Evie assumed that the family connection had made Loulou a little soft when it came to the boy.

When James arrived back downstairs, he found the group all sitting around Ops on various chairs, sofas, cushions and rugs. Evie, was now cross-legged on the floor, casually leaning one arm on the dog who could speak. The dog did not seem to notice, and was in conversation with Grandma. Artemis, who was now up and about – if still fragile – was resting on the sofa and Mr T had taken a place on the arm of the empty chair. James went and sat in the chair with his cat. He still thought of Mr T as 'his cat', in much the same way – he imagined – that Mr T thought of James as 'his boy.' Grandad was perched on the tall seat beside the computer. Grandma, on the sofa, was leaning forward to concentrate.

"James!" She called out. "Good. We waited for you, dear. I didn't realise you hadn't quite finished your introductions. This is Agent Loulou," she gestured towards the enormous dog who was stretched out along the rug, head resting on her forelegs, "And I gather you met Probationary Agent Evie." James nodded. "Agent Loulou thought you might find it instructive to be involved in our debrief – so you just sit there and listen, and take it all in, shall you?"

James nodded again.

Despite the assortment of seats, everything felt very formal. He had become quite used to life at his grandparents' house and was comfortable there. Now, with these strangers, everything had changed. His grandparents seemed suddenly very business-like and he felt oddly shy.

James knew quite a lot about Lifelink now, but it had still all seemed very much like a game. It was fun dealing with the animals – like a story, where he was the main character, with this '*Dr Dolittle*' ability to speak to some of his animal friends. It was his own special world that no-one else, no-one in the real world anyway, knew about.

These newcomers had changed all that.

James could clearly see now that his grandparents were part of a much bigger organisation, with James watching what was going on from the sidelines. James understood that this had always been the case, and that his feelings of resentment were unreasonable, but he had very much liked being the centre of his Grandparents' world.

"James, you are just as important in the wider scheme of things, too," Mr T suddenly whispered. "Just as we all are. Wait and see."

James was startled and glanced across at Mr T, who was sitting still – not even looking at James. He appeared to be on the verge of sleep, but James knew he was in fact concentrating hard on what was going on around him. Mr T never ceased to amaze James with his cleverness.

James abruptly realised that he had not been paying attention to the conversation, and tuned back in, to hear Artemis conclude her story of kidnap and rescue.

"So, here I am, much improved I have to say. Alive and functional. Ready to get back to work in fact – perhaps you could tell Agent Singh that for me? He seems to think I need some time out."

"Right, then." This gruff voice was from Loulou, who seemed to ignore Artemis's last comment. "And you can't remember anything about the base you were taken to? Other than the general vicinity?"

"No," Artemis was suddenly speaking in a whisper. "I just ran, and I shouldn't have. I should have taken a good look around, got something – a house number, a road name, something. I was … I was really frightened." Artemis was not meeting anyone's gaze as her voice trailed off.

"Hey, come on now," said Grandad, leaning towards her. "You did just about the bravest thing I ever heard of. You had no idea if there would be an escape route up those stairs, but you took your chance anyway – with a Doberman no less! You have absolutely nothing to reproach yourself for, agent. You did a first class job."

"Yes, of course," said Loulou. "No argument there, but we don't have a lot to go on." She paused, doing a good impression of a frown. "Of course, if they *think* we know where it was, they'll have moved anyway. So, in a way, we've lost nothing. Those hawks will have reported back by now, so they know you got through. I don't see how we can trace the cell's whereabouts though ..."

The group was silent each one trying to think through the problem. James took a deep breath and spoke, very quietly.

"I suppose, we can't just – ask a badger, where this Titan is?"

He had been very afraid to speak, as he had a feeling that this seemingly obvious solution would already have been raised, unless there was a good reason why it couldn't be done. But, as he didn't know the reason himself, he decided to swallow the lump in his throat and speak up. James unconsciously pressed himself further into his chair, as five pairs of eyes turned to study him. Grandad cleared his throat.

"Yes, that would be the best thing in an ideal world, but it's, er, problematic. Badgers –" Grandad seemed to consider what he could say on the subject. "Badgers. They're. Well, for a start, they're not friendly –"

Loulou "hrmphed" from her position on the rug and Evie adjusted her legs as if they were getting cramped.

"They're vicious," said Artemis, with a shudder. "And usually they don't speak. Not to us anyway."

Mr T cracked opened his eyelids and spoke, in his steady, purring voice:

"Some animals either don't, or can't, speak to each other. Cats and badgers, for instance. Hrrr. Perhaps the most interesting thing about Artemis's account is that she communicated with a badger at all." Artemis shuddered again, while Mr T went on. "Badgers are hunters who have themselves been hunted, by man, for centuries. They hold the biggest grudge you can imagine. Foxes, the same. Badgers detest humans, as a rule, and any animal that consorts with humans – like cats and dogs. Yet here we have one who not only talks to cats but has at least one man – two if we count Newman, maybe even more – working for him, as well as dogs. Hrrr. It was thought that badgers could not understand creaturespeak between any but a very few woodland species. None of us ever met anyone who had actually spoken to one. Until now, hrrr?" He inclined his head respectfully towards Artemis. "It is possible that we have been very wrong about them in the past."

"But still," interrupted Agent Loulou. "If badgers can be understood more widely, wouldn't *someone* have heard them before now? I think maybe it's just one badger. Maybe one badger can speak to other species. I know that's not how it works but I can't see any other explanation."

"So, anyway," Grandad turned back to James. "If you want to speak to a badger, you have to do it the hard way. From canine, to fox, to badger. Except of course foxes don't like dogs –"

"And I don't trust foxes either," said Artemis.

The group lapsed into a troubled silence once again.

"There are Misant humans," James said, aloud, surprising himself again. He carried on, before he could think about it too much. "I'm just saying – it could be anyone really. Instead of a badger I mean. You just need to talk to a Misant." Another thought struck him. "Do they ever," James searched for the word he wanted, "change sides?"

"Defect?" Grandma said. "Sometimes. That's what we always hope for, that's what we try to get people to do. So, yes, there have been a few ... Could that help us Agent Loulou?" Grandma smiled at James and he felt less nervous.

"Anyone who had defected wouldn't be up-to-date," Loulou said. "And, of course, they'll have been debriefed already. They're not agents, they're just members of Lifelink. I'm not sure they'd be up to undercover work - if that's what you're suggesting?"

James felt he wasn't getting very far with his suggestions but, all the same, he was starting to relax and enjoy being a small part of the group. He could hear the reassuring sound of Mr T purring quietly beside him.

Evie had been following the conversation intently but without joining in. She suddenly spoke up though, surprising even herself.

"We have undercover agents?" Evie addressed Loulou who, as her tutor, she felt should have imparted this sort of knowledge earlier.

"Mmn, not as such," Loulou said. "We have done in the past but, as a rule, we don't think it's worth the risk. They have no scruples, Misants. If the agent is uncovered, it goes badly, always. We have a few observers though. They masquerade as non-speakers, but they listen, and they report back anything they overhear."

"We track the chatter," Agent Zed said. "Anything seems a bit odd gets logged on the system. If we get a lot of unusual comments or events in one particular area we send in an investigator."

The boy, James, piped up again.

"What sort of things do they investigate, Grand – Agent Zed?" Evie let her mouth twitch at the corner, and she watched Agent Em's do the same. Zed hesitated, saying:

"I think we might be getting a bit off track here. Agent Loulou has her mission to consider – which is to trace this leadership cell." Evie saw James' face fall. So, it seemed, did Agent Zed because he continued: "But in a nutshell, if they can, Misants will undermine anything – from the car of a well-placed human, to corrupting the results of a medical trial. I can give you examples later, James, of things for which the Misants take credit. But just now we need to concentrate on finding this cell."

By lunch time, Evie could see that everyone was tired, and no way forward had yet been agreed. Loulou said she needed some fresh air and to stretch her legs, so she and Evie excused themselves and headed for a stroll outside. They passed a One-Stop and Evie bought some sandwiches to share as they walked. They strolled slowly along the edges of a playing field, skirting the lines of the football pitches.

"What do you think of the boy?" Loulou said.

"Not much," Evie said, dismissively.

"I'm not so sure," Loulou rumbled, as if considering. "He's still a youngster, but he asked some good questions in there, and I can't help but think that is the way we may have to go."

"Sorry, what way?" Evie had no idea what it was that Loulou was suggesting.

"Undercover..." Loulou's voice had gone very quiet, and she sounded unsure of herself – something Evie had never heard from her teacher before now. "To tell you the truth, I was considering it too, when James raised the problem of communication with the Misant movement. Like Singh said, if they're abducting Lifelink agents in broad daylight, attacking in the open, if badgers have started communicating – well, it has to mean *some*thing." Loulou came to a stop and faced Evie, in full teacher mode. "Up until now the Misants have been a fairly low-level movement, upsetting things where they could – not doing a bad job of it sometimes – but there's been nothing really big. If they are suddenly planning an operation that's large enough for them to risk exposure, then we – Lifelink – need to know about it, fast." Loulou lapsed into silence, her eyebrows rumpled.

"Lou?" Evie dragged Loulou out of her thoughts. "This undercover gig … Who, exactly?"

"Well, that *is* the question," agreed Loulou, turning back towards Ops and picking up the pace. Evie jogged along beside her, thinking.

CHAPTER 17

MR T'S SECRET

J AMES HAD HEADED up to his room while his grandparents tidied up downstairs after lunch. He had decided to play a new game for a bit – he was still choosing whether to be an elf or a gnome. He had meant to level up over the holidays, so he could play online with kids from school. The summer holidays ended the week before though, and James celebrated his twelfth birthday - on the third of September - with Mum and his grandparents at the cinema.

Over the summer, he had spent just one day with his year six friends. He had felt very awkward because he couldn't tell them anything about what he had been doing and all he really wanted was to get back to Ops.

Now, of course, they weren't even going to the same secondary school, and he had messaged them less and less. His online school had begun its autumn term and he had immediately decided he enjoyed being educated in a chat room with teachers he called by their first names. It was odd and very cool. The other kids in his classes were just names on the screen, but they got to know one another through their conversations, and they were almost as real to James now as his former classmates in primary school had been. They tended to live in far-off places, like Singapore, and presumably had parents who travelled for work. One lived on a mountain that was so isolated there was no other school he could attend. It was all fascinating – yet another secret window to a different world. There were remarkably few classes, and only four school days, each week – although the tutors were available to answer questions by email at any time. The classes were limited too: no drama, no art and of course no technical subjects. But James didn't mind. His new tablet, his main birthday present from his grandparents, was brilliant and – all in all – he thought dropping out of regular school was turning out to be a great move.

Thinking about school pricked his conscience and he put the game away, to pick up the tablet and start his Maths homework. Everyone downstairs was waiting for Agents Loulou and Evie to reappear, at which point some sort of decision had to be made. James was just finishing the last question when he heard voices from the kitchen and realised the agents had returned. He popped in his working out, and the answer, before closing the screen and racing downstairs.

Mr T had a secret. He had known it for several days now, but he was not sure when was the right time to share it. Mr T knew many things. He knew, for instance, that Helen was perfectly correct when she accused Em of having an ulterior motive in presenting James with Mr T. Zed and Em had been meeting up with Mr T over the years to keep track of Helen's and James' well-being. The pair had admitted to Mr T that they missed them both dreadfully when they agreed to go their separate ways so, knowing Mr T was there, gave James' grandparents great comfort. There had been more to his mission than that, however.

Mr T had talked to James every day since his arrival at Rowan Avenue, when he was barely out of kittenhood but already well briefed in his duties.

James had, of course, also been talking to Mr T. Mr T had found their one-sided conversations frustrating, when James had failed to hear certain pieces of excellent advice for instance, but Mr T felt all his endeavours had been rewarded the morning James finally heard him speak.

Mr T's newest secret, however, was concerned with none of these events. It had to do with the fact that his communication with James had, quite unexpectedly, just improved no end.

James arrived downstairs just as the group reconvened in the living room. He seated himself on the bottom stair, from where he could watch and listen. Agent Loulou had the floor, literally. He listened closely to her deep, warm, growl of a voice as it rumbled out of the room.

"I do miss Jake's unique talents. In a situation like this, he would have been invaluable. We could have gone *near* to the Misant base and he would have picked up *something* at least. Failing that, he could have spoken with a neutral - maybe a fox or stoat - and gained some second-hand intel. As it is, we are stuck with speaking face-to-face, or not at all – which is hardly an option. I would like to propose, therefore, that I myself take on the mission, solo and undercover."

The noise following Agent Loulou's statement was impressive for such a small group. James took in some of it: that Agent Loulou was suggesting something far too risky; that she could not undertake a mission without backup; that she was being too optimistic about its possible success. Agent Loulou waited patiently for the uproar to subside. "Unless anyone has a better idea," she huffed.

The room was as quiet now as it had been noisy before. After a moment or two, James heard Mr T's distinctive purring tones.

"I have some information that could possibly be relevant, hrrr."

James watched as everyone turned towards Mr T, with expressions suggesting surprise, doubt or interest.

"Jake's particular gift," Mr T said. Then he paused.

"Yes?" barked Agent Loulou.

"It may not be entirely lost ... hrrr?" Mr T said.

"What on Earth do you mean, T?" said Zed. "Be more specific."

"It may have continued, in his son." It took a while for the sentence to hit home, then six pairs of eyes were gradually turned to fix on James, where he sat half hidden by the banisters. James felt his mind go blank and said:

"I don't know what he means?"

Mr T coughed a little and carried on.

"James, my apologies. I had not intended to spring that on you, hrrr. It may have been better to talk to you first, in private, but here we are."

"I still don't know what you mean," James complained, feeling even less comfortable now than he had earlier at the beginning of the meeting.

"No." Mr T sounded irritated. "No, you don't. Agents, James can communicate sub-verbally, hrrr. But he is not, himself, aware of it."

There was a sucking in and blowing out of breath throughout the group until Grandma demanded:

"How do you know?"

"I have spoken with him. And I might add that I cannot speak sub-verbally normally, so the talent must belong to James ... James?"

"Yes?"

"Do you remember a brief conversation you and I had earlier in Ops, hrrr? Not to go into too much detail, but one in which you were somewhat concerned by recent developments and the possibility that they might in some way, hrrr, exclude you?"

"Ye-es…" James said, feeling his ears start to tingle.

"Would it surprise you very much to know that, during that conversation, I did not actually speak?"

"Yes, you did!" said James. "You basically told me not to worry!"

"Quite correct," agreed Mr T. "But I did not in fact say that out loud, hrrr. And if you take a moment, perhaps you will remember that you did not speak out loud either."

The warmth in James' ears subsided, giving way to a cold feeling that slid down from his shoulders to his middle back and made him shudder.

"He's right. I … I didn't." James said.

Grandma and Grandad were exchanging a look that made James feel as though they were also speaking sub-verbally. He couldn't decide, though, if they looked hopeful or concerned.

"Well now," Agent Loulou woofed. "That *is* interesting!"

"It is," said Grandad. "And it is also untested and requires considerable thought. I think we should take some time out. I need time to talk to people – HQ obviously ... and, Helen."

"Excuse me," said James from the stairs. "Could someone please explain this to me a bit more?" He waited for an answer, lips clamped together.

Evie whispered, quite loudly, to Loulou.

"So, he doesn't know *any*thing?" Loulou shot Evie a look, that James could see clearly told her to 'shut up,' then stood up and shook herself.

"Right you are Zed, Evie and I will be off. We have a place for tonight, courtesy of Co-Ordinator Kath – not far. We'll see you in the morning." Loulou herded Evie out of the room and the front door thudded shut behind them. Artemis stood up too, saying, in her nasal tones that always made James think of the kazoo he used to play as a child:

"I, er, I think I'll go for a bit of a stroll – get this leg moving again. I've been sitting far too long."

"Yes, thank you, agent," said Grandma. "See you in, say, half an hour?"

Artemis hopped down from the sofa, landing perfectly on her new leg, and disappeared. James heard the swoosh of the cat flap as Grandma gestured towards the armchair where Evie had been sitting.

"Come and make yourself comfortable, James. I need to explain something more about your Dad.

Zed, while I do that, perhaps you'd give Helen a call? Ask her over for supper."

Mr T padded quietly over to join James, curling up on his lap like a warm, furry, cushion.

CHAPTER 18

THE MISANT VIEW

AS DAWN CREPT over the horizon and gentle rays of sunlight started to pick out colour, in the clearing known as Badgers Copse, anyone seeking traces of a Harris hawk would have been disappointed. The ground was grassy and clear, except for insects and wild plants. Not so much as a feather was left to identify the spot where a hawk had fallen.

After punishing the hawk and instructing the man to gather more information, Titan had killed and eaten a hedgehog, then returned to his familiar sett. His sleeping chamber, freshly cleaned and lined with hay and bracken, was filled with the scent of home that linked him directly to his ancestors. They had built this sett countless generations before.

It had eight entrances and various chambers for sleeping or birthing and, as a cub, Titan had first heard stories of his ancestry from within these dark and comforting walls. Now, he was the leader, and he passed on those same history lessons to his own cubs – just as they would to theirs in time.

This evening Defender, his lifemate, had ushered three of the cubs who were nearly two seasons old into the largest chamber. Titan was to speak to them of their heritage. They were old enough to understand. Defender had heard him teach this lesson more times than there were seasons in a generation of litters, but he watched her settle down across the chamber entrance with complete patience, to hear the tale again. The three cubs calmed themselves, in imitation of their mother, and Titan began to speak. His voice reverberated through the clay walls, strong and warm, like a rock in summer.

"Yarrow. Ragwort. Speedwell." Each cub looked up in turn and did not look away. "The words I give to you today, you will remember. The story I tell, you will remember. This knowledge will nest in your hearts and you will carry it like a cub, and you will remember. We, badgers, own all woodland. We live with the woods, we shelter with the woods, the wood is our home as the sett is our home. We have outlasted the wolves, who once preyed on our kind.

But now, our enemy is fearsome. Our enemy is the human. Our enemy will stalk you in your dreams and kill you when you wake. Despite this, we will continue beyond humans, as we continue beyond wolves. Humans are no more to us than rotten bark. They no more deserve our respect than a dead tree deserves leaves. It is the humans who brought cattle to the edges of our woodlands. Their cattle brought the plague. The illness that weakens our breath and kills. Not only with this do humans kill us."

"With dogs!" This was Yarrow, the biggest of the three cubs, who had been edging closer to Titan as if drawn in by the story. Titan noticed how Yarrow's stocky build resembled Defender in her younger days. He felt a surge, like something reaching out from inside his chest, and recognised the strong connection from the cub before him to his own past.

"Yes, cub. Men hunt us, using dogs and sticks that throw killing pellets. They have no battle honour; they do not meet their prey in combat. They are worse than the wolves. We have taken the lives of dogs, and some have fought bravely and we honour their deaths. Men kill without battle. This is what sets men apart from all other people. Men are foul, like the plague they carry." Titan was pleased to note that every cub was lying its snout on the chamber floor in the mark of agreement. He allowed himself to sit too, head raised. "The word for this most shameful of killing is 'cull'. Learn this word well, cubs. It comes to us from the humans themselves, for we have no word that carries such disgrace. No people have. Lodge this word deep within your hearts and swear vengeance against it. Without vengeance, humans will cull whole families, group after group, using their stone sticks to destroy us." Titan also knew the word 'rifle' but chose not to use more words out loud than he had to, from the specifically human realm, when in conversation with creaturekind. "They trap us, kill us, and leave our setts bare. No sett must ever fall cold, cubs. Our history, our memories, our ancestors, all hold within the sett. The sett is our home, our mother, our past. If men destroy a family, the next family *must* join themselves to that sett, so that warmth can keep their breath and scents alive. We will not let the memory grow cold. This is the badger way, the honourable way. We do this, and we continue. We do this, and we will survive Men. The woodlands are ours cubs, as they have been, as they are, as they will be when the moon rises again."

Titan raised himself to his feet and the cubs copied him. Defender moved behind them and nudged them gently back out of the chamber. Titan knew she would repeat his words to them, every dusk, until they lodged in the cubs' hearts. He brushed Defender's side as she passed, sharing her scent, and she made a small churring noise in return: *it is well.*

Alone again, Titan still dwelled on the problem at hand. He knew that men's urge to destroy extended to many different species across the Earth, that some had even been completely wiped out – he knew this from the Misant network that reached across the seas to places he could not, and did not even wish to, imagine. Now though, men were threatening to wipe out *his* species. It seemed to Titan that he could no longer distance himself from the war that had persisted quietly around the world for years. Despite what he told the cubs, he doubted that surviving the culling would be enough. He was very afraid that, with this enemy, it would be the badgers who lost. It was the unthinkable, yet it had fallen to him to think it. If Misants of all species were acting against humans, then Titan was going to ensure that action was effective – even when that meant talking with men to use them against their own kind. Titan would think the unthinkable, and do the unthinkable, because woodlands of setts would never be allowed to fall cold while he – or any of his line – breathed the twilight air.

The Stranger was not nocturnal, but he paid little attention to the passing of day to night, as many of those with whom he dealt were. He simply slept when the opportunity arose, like the soldier he was.

The Stranger had always inhabited a world where the people on the planet were not limited to the eight or so billion humans, but included the far more numerous lives of all those creatures who shared this precarious home. He knew, from the many hundred species with which he could communicate, that all lives had the same drive to survive, all played a role in the vast organic machine of Earth, and most had hopes and fears.

He had lived on the planet many years, sharing the thoughts of everyone around him when he chose and listening to what was, to him, the verbal heartbeat of the world. He and all those lives were part of the same massive biological organ, growing, reproducing, dying and being renewed – as it had for thousands of years and should for thousands more.

As he grew up, however, he had gradually become aware of a cancer within the world, far more serious than the ailments that occasionally endangered a species here and there, or rearranged a continent or two. It was as if he, and everyone around him, was a single cell in the living world – but some cells had mutated and now threatened the life of the whole. These dangerous cells were, predominantly, human. They multiplied and threatened more and more of the Earth. He had known for years that the only way to save the planet, and all life, was to cut out and destroy the cancerous cells to allow nature the chance to heal itself.

It was upsetting that the rot had begun with men. The Stranger did not see a vast difference between species – he saw personalities rather than genus - but still, the cancer had begun with his own kind. He would have felt a responsibility regardless, simply as a thinking element within the world, but the fact that the destruction had begun with humans, and was still led by them, caused him no little pain.

Every day, humans who chose to, could read about new disasters. About whole species hunted to extinction or killed by a virus imported by boat or plane. Things that nature would have kept apart, man slammed together and ignored the consequences. Humans spent immense amounts of time developing weapons that either allowed them to render whole tracts of the Earth lifeless for centuries, or to systematically kill humans and other animals, allowing them no chance at defence.

Humans said nature was 'cruel', but nature was an angel compared to mankind. Nature allowed the spread of disease, encouraged combat, developed hunters and prey. But nature's destruction generally led to new life. It was a cycle that fuelled itself and made the planet stronger and better - each creature adapting to find food, warmth, shelter, in ways that fit together so complicatedly that human naturalists had barely begun to touch the surface of their interdependency.

Not so men. Humans destroyed on a gigantic scale, with no forethought, no reason, for nothing but personal gain.

There were, it was true, people within human society who had noticed what was happening to the world. But they were like coma patients, struggling up towards sensibility, starting to form words and ideas but not yet able to form a clear picture. As far as the Stranger could see, things were out of control.

The Earth would be plummeting to its doom long before the rest of mankind realised it needed to take action or be obliterated. The Earth was being forced into a path that would soon be too far advanced for humans to remedy its course. The only remedy, therefore, was to stop the humans themselves - the destroyers, the cancerous cells.

The Misant organisation had of course been trying to do exactly this for well over a century. The Stranger was not the first to recognise the problem. But it was a disparate organisation, disorganised. It eschewed the technology it despised and blamed, communicating by more traditional means. It had contented itself with disrupting where it could, with guerrilla tactics, trying to slow down the human world and give those who realised the problem the chance to effect a change. But it wasn't working, because people were too stupid, too slow.

Things were getting worse. They spilled oil into the sea; they fished the sea bare; they re-routed rivers and moved animals all over the world; they created carbon emissions and strewed garbage wherever they lived; they cut down the very trees that allowed the planet to breathe. If they did not directly kill another species, they ruined its habitat so it died anyway. They upset the balance of life that had been developing since the world began.

And they did it all in the space of a century or so.

It was cruelly, utterly shocking, yet even worse was the reason for their destruction. All of it, all of it was for their personal comfort. Because mankind wanted their brief span on Earth to be physically convenient. Because they wanted to eat without having to hunt or plant. Because they wanted warmth in winter and to be cool in summer. Because they wanted an easy, quick way to travel that did not involve any effort. They wanted comfort – and they took it, at the expense of billions of lives including, eventually, their own. The planet was dying – for no more reason than greed.

Seven years ago, the Stranger had set himself the single task of rising up through the Misant chain of command in order that he could ensure the success of his personal mission - to lead, and drive, the Misant forces.

Once he was in charge, he could influence Misant action throughout the country, thereby demonstrating to other Misants across the world what could be achieved. Now he was second in command to only one, in the whole of England, and that Misant's name was Titan.

CHAPTER 19

HELEN~~'~~S VIEW

WHEN MUM ENTERED the kitchen, James was helping Grandma by tipping a bag of pasta into a saucepan of boiling water, something Mum would never have allowed him to do unsupervised. He looked up as she came in, in time to see her quickly change her expression, from shock, to a smile.

"Hi Mum." James grinned. "Did you bring my clean pyjamas?"

She assured him she had, as well as bringing with her a bottle of elderflower wine, a fruit salad and a pot of double cream to help out with supper.

James had been living between the two houses, after Mum returned home, keeping belongings at both. Despite having settled in so well, James had been a little homesick at Cromwell Street. He had missed the way Mum prepared his lunches, and seemed to know when he was thirsty, or which T-shirt he wanted to wear that day. At his grandparents', he had to sort himself out most of the time. In a way, he enjoyed it, being treated more like an adult – and, of course, the Lifelink work was brilliant. But he still missed the way Mum always asked after his day and how he was feeling. Now though, James truly had the best of both worlds.

As they sat down, Mr T joined them by curling up on the nearby windowsill, which was a good height for participating in the conversation. Artemis was enjoying her own supper in a corner of the kitchen. Grandma had been poaching fresh fish every day for her since her operation, and Artemis's appetite had soon returned. They sat down to supper and Grandad raised his glass.

"I would like to propose a toast! To James, a very talented member of the Doughty clan." They all took a sip, and James saw Mum turn towards Grandad like she had a question, but Grandad was still talking. "Helen, something has happened, and we thought we should take a little time this evening to discuss its implications."

"So, this is not just supper," Mum said. "I did think it was a bit short notice. What on Earth has happened now?"

They waited, watching while Grandad finished chewing a mouthful of pasta, before he explained.

"Mr T has made a discovery."

"Oh, that's right, blame me," James heard a quiet voice from the windowsill.

"About James' creaturespeak abilities," Grandad said. "I'm not sure how much you knew about Jake's talent? I know you and he tried to keep the worlds somewhat … separate. For very good reasons."

James was studying his supper plate and eating quietly. He wasn't at all sure Mum would find the new discovery quite as exciting as he did himself.

"It's fine, Zedekiah." Mum smiled. "Jake and I did make that decision, and we did it for James, as you know. But things have changed now."

Grandad speared a tomato and then held it in the air on its way to his mouth, while he spoke.

"I'm not sure you knew Jake could speak sub-verbally?"

"You mean telepathically?" Mum said. "The fact that I disliked him bringing his work home didn't mean that we wouldn't sometimes talk about it. He used to say that he wished he and I could speak that way as it could save a lot of time! But I think we did pretty well without it..." James thought Mum sounded a bit sad and reached out to squeeze her fingers, raising a gentle smile on her face. Suddenly, though, her head whipped round to stare directly at her son. "You mean … *James?*"

"Yes, I do."

Grandma, who had been working steadily through the contents of her supper plate, put down her water glass saying:

"It doesn't change anything. He's still eleven."

"Twelve!" James corrected.

"Twelve," said Grandma, "and therefore still a minor. We're not even sure what the extent of his talent *is* yet."

Grandma reached across and rubbed Mum's other hand reassuringly where it was lying on the table, her fork on the untouched plate. James quickly released the hand he was holding, as he thought Mum ought to at least have one free to eat supper.

"But you had something in mind, didn't you?" Mum sat back in her chair and folded her arms.

 "You always were sharp my dear." Grandma smiled, in a friendly way. "There is a problem, a tactical problem. If James' talent is indeed the same as Jake's, then it would be a godsend to us right now. But James is a child, one whose talent is untested. It would be useful to find out if he can talk to more species." Grandma stopped. James' mum said nothing, but suddenly seemed to remember she was supposed to be eating supper, and popped some pasta into her mouth.

James glanced at all the adults in turn, trying to work out what was going on. He felt he ought to be part of this conversation, given it was all about him, but he didn't understand it all.

Give it a moment, said Mr T. *Just listen. If you have any questions, we can go over them together, later.*

Except, of course, he didn't say it aloud.

Mum sucked a deep breath in through her nose and broke the silence.

"Jake told me a few things about Lifelink, and about creaturespeak. Some of them he probably shouldn't have told a non-speaker, non-operative, but now I doubt that matters." She had neatly replaced her cutlery and pushed her plate away a little, to lean forwards as she spoke. "I understand that sub-verbal speaking is an extremely rare thing. Jake didn't know of anyone else in his generation of operatives who could do it. I assume you haven't found anyone since, or we wouldn't be having this conversation. I know that, because of his particular ability, Jake was sent on more missions than most agents and he was almost always selected for the more dangerous ones. I know he was on just such a mission when he disappeared. Oh, and of course I know about Misants. Now, would I be correct in saying that – despite all this – you would like James to follow in his father's footsteps?"

Grandad was shifting in his seat while Grandma studied the plate in front of her. James had to admit that, the way Mum put it, it all sounded very bad. Grandad looked up, his face brightening.

"If James were to … follow that path, he would never do so alone. Jake, you recall, was on a solo mission and out of contact?"

"Of course he wouldn't!" Mum practically exploded. "He is twelve!" She screwed her paper napkin into a ball, and dropped it onto her half-eaten supper.

The group fell quiet again. James felt an uncomfortable lump somewhere in his chest and, despite Mr T's earlier warning, decided to speak up.

"Mum?"

She blinked and focussed on James as if she had almost forgotten he was at the table.

"Yes dear?" She sighed.

"Is Grandma suggesting I should become a Lifelink agent, like Dad?"

Grandma, he noticed, was pink near her cheekbones.

"I rather think she is," Mum said. "But, of course, you're much too young, yet. You have schooling, and a lot of growing up to do before you make that sort of decision. But…" She seemed to struggle to find her words. "But, I did agree that you could help your grandparents, and now you are involved in *that* world it is highly unlikely you're going to choose to be a … a software engineer." She smiled briefly. "Maybe you can help out in *some* way, but I am going to want to know all about it beforehand. And - make no mistake young man - I still have the final say, on everything, right up until you're eighteen."

James slowly took in the fact that Mum was allowing him to help. The lumpy feeling disappeared with a shiver of excitement.

"We can try out his speaking ability then? Let him meet a few people?" Grandad said.

James' Mum gave him a flat smile that didn't reach her eyes, but did soften her face a bit.

"Yes. I really do want my son to do what he is meant to do. To make the most of *all* his talents. But I will also look out for him – don't think I won't. I know you think the world of him. But I *also* know you'd do anything for Lifelink - and, as a matter of fact, I understand that too. I still think what you're all doing may be the most important thing anyone on *Earth* is doing. It's just that … my *son* comes first, the rest of the world second."

Grandma looked up at her saying:

"Just as it should, my dear."

"Anyway!" James' Mum smiled again, properly this time. "I had a bit of news of my own to share. I've handed in my resignation, which is why I'm not yet back at school."

"Oh!" Grandma and Grandad looked immediately guilty and James felt his own face mirroring theirs. James had completely missed the fact that the term had started, yet Mum had not gone back to work, even though he had been living at home some of the time.

"Oh!" James said. "I didn't think!"

Mum laughed, and Grandad shrugged his shoulders, holding his hands up while Grandma flicked at him with her napkin.

"Don't worry," Mum said. "It means I get to surprise you all now."

"What are you doing instead?" asked Grandad.

"I'm going back to veterinary work. There are plenty of adverts for nurses locally. I only moved to the school to be near James and help him out. I would have stayed, if things had been ... different. I did like White Oaks Primary and I'll miss it but, honestly, I miss the animals more!"

"Quite understandable, hrrr." Mr T rumbled, joining in from the window. Though Mum, of course, didn't know.

Grandma clapped her hands happily and said:

"Well I, for one, think that's excellent. You're a natural, Helen. Jake said if he didn't know better he'd think you *could* speak to them. In fact, he wondered why you didn't study for your vet qualification. I know you said it didn't appeal. But you could still consider it."

"Oh, I'm not sure about that," Mum said. "Sounds like a lot of hard work and study - and I've got James. I *like* being a nurse. You get more of the good stuff and none of the heart-breaking decisions!" The conversation carried on around the subject for a little while, until James started yawning and Mum gently suggested that it might be time for him to head upstairs.

"I'll come up for a hug before I go," she said.

"That's OK." James nipped round the table and gave her a quick hug where she sat. "You carry on chatting with Grandma and Grandad. See you tomorrow Mum!"

James trudged slowly up the stairs, feeling very sleepy, full from supper and excited about tomorrow - all at once.

Mr T slipped quietly down from the windowsill ready to pad up the stairs after James. He had not forgotten his promise to answer any questions James might still have.

"My little boy, growing up," he heard Helen say.

"Helen?" Agent Em said, her tone suggesting a change of subject.

Mr T paused, curious. "Have you actually applied for any positions yet?"

"No, I was going to start at the weekend. Why?"

Em glanced at Zed.

"I had an idea, but I didn't want to mention it while James was around, to give you chance to say 'no', but …. why don't you work here?"

"Huh?" Helen said. "Here? In your house? Doing what, Emma?"

"As a veterinary nurse. Heaven knows I could do with the help. Both strays and operatives are brought in, as you know. James, bless, has been lovely. But he's no trained nurse."

"Oh, Emma," said Helen, "It's not just something to occupy myself: I have to pay the bills." She flexed her shoulders up and down.

Zed chuckled, saying:

"But, sweetheart, how do you think Em and I pay the bills?"

Helen frowned. Mr T curled up on the bottom stair to hear the rest.

"I don't know. I've never thought about it!" Helen said. "Pensions I suppose?"

Zed laughed loudly, throwing his head back.

"They'd have to be pretty good pensions to pay for that Harley, never mind the trips up and down country, the medical supplies for Em. And the food! No, dear girl, we are *paid* for our work. Lifelink operatives get salaries, just like everyone else. MI5 doesn't expect its agents to work for nothing, and neither does our organisation."

Mr T noticed that Helen's cheeks were a darker pink.

"Jake was freelancing, though, wasn't he? As well as his missions. I just never asked how much they paid him for that. I never thought …" Helen trailed off. "And we still get some extra money to help out, from his investments." She shook her head. "Were those made by Lifelink, for us, not by Jake?"

"Yes," Zed agreed quietly.

"Why on *Earth* didn't you tell me?"

"Because," Zed said. "You were rather anti-Lifelink at the time."

Helen didn't respond.

"So," said Em. "What *do* you think, then?"

"I don't know," Helen said.

"Right, I've put you on the spot," said Em. "Don't decide now. Whatever you choose is fine by us - no pressure either way. Now, would you like another coffee?"

"Yes!" said Helen. The agents, startled, both stared at her. "Yes," she repeated. "I *would* like to work here! Oh – and a coffee – yes please, that would be great too."

Mr T stood up and stretched, planning to give James the good news. Artemis, who had been snoozing on a spare dining chair, opened one eye to hiss at him:

"*Really?* A member of *Ops,* who doesn't creaturespeak *a word?* At least she'll be good for … security… ?" Mr T purred happily on his way upstairs, leaving Artemis mewing to herself: *"Humans…"*

CHAPTER 20

AN UNEXPECTED
DEVELOPMENT

AGENT SINGH READ, then re-read, the communication he had just received from Ops West. As he did so, his face took on a greyish undertone. The gist of the information was that *fifteen* separate operatives in an area of Gloucestershire had reported hearing Misant communications that variously included words such as: 'infiltration', 'timing', and 'operation.'

"Michiko?" Agent Singh's voice was hard as a bullet as he gripped the phone.

"Yes, sir," came the sharp response.

"Michiko, what's going on? I just got the report. Either it's so big that too many Misants are involved to keep it quiet - or, they're so confident of success they're not even *trying* to keep off the radar. Have you identified the threat yet?"

"Ash and Sheera are out in the field now, sir, doing just that – I hope."

"What have you got up there?"

"Quite a lot. Chemicals, pharmaceuticals, food and drink of course, polymer research, you name it. We've got flammable industries - oil and gas - and poisonable factories," was the grim response. "Agent Singh, whatever is planned appears to be an operation on a scale larger than anything we've seen from them yet. I would actually really appreciate some back-up to try to narrow down the options."

"Of course," Singh said. "I have some people in mind. I'll be in touch again inside an hour." Singh was already replacing the handset as Agent Michiko's voice ended the call with:

"Yes, sir."

He picked it straight back up, and had begun dialling, when his attention was caught by his computer screen - where an email had just appeared, flagged urgent, from Ops South.

James was sitting on the edge of a bench in the park watching Agent Loulou plodding up and down - impatiently James felt. Agent Evie was slumped -

half on half off the other end of the bench - with her arms folded, facing away from him. James wished his companions were friendlier. He knew this was a test of sorts and he didn't want to let anyone down.

It was a damp morning and a grey one. James hoped the rain would hold off as he didn't much fancy sitting on a bench getting soaked waiting for creatures that, if they had any sense, would stay in the dry instead.

His eyes felt scratchy through lack of sleep, and tiredness made him notice the cold, gritty feel of the bench seat and the itch of an insect bite on his ankle. He rubbed it with the trainer of his opposite foot and thought how Evie might take the trouble to at least talk to him while Loulou roamed around.

He was about to say this when there was a loud 'shushing' noise, and a dark blur swept down just over his head, to land on the grass a short distance from of his trainers. James, who had ducked, sat back up. A round, black, bead-like eye studied him from a sleek, black head cocked sideways. James was not sure if this was a rook or a crow but, whatever it was, it was considerably bigger than the blackbirds in his garden at home. James stared back and blinked.

"Well?" croaked the bird. "I was under the impression I was here for a reason?"

"Oh!" James said.

Evie turned around to face the bird.

"You'll have to forgive him, he's only really spoken to cats."

"Haaa," said the bird. "Well, if this is your first time out, I am happy to now inform you that you can also speak to corvids."

"To what?" said James.

The bird angled its large grey beak downwards and peered up, towards James, for all the world like a librarian.

"Corvids," he repeated. "That is not a type of bird, it is a genus: *corvus* to be exact. It is a family that includes rooks, like myself, but also crows, jackdaws and ravens. You may expect to converse easily with any of these. You might also be able to speak to jays, magpies and choughs. As for the rest of the bird population, I'm afraid I cannot say."

"Oh," said James, again. "That's actually pretty great."

"Charmed, I'm sure," the rook said and, giving a nod to Evie, left.

Evie laughed.

"What?" James said.

Evie swallowed and controlled herself enough to speak.

"It's just – great first conversation."

"That wasn't my first conversation!" said James. "I've been talking loads with Mr T – and Artemis."

"Sure. But that was your first corvid. I think he'll remember you. I mean, you didn't even thank him for turning up!"

James felt his face go hot, realising that the annoying girl was right. He had forgotten his manners. He supposed they were just as important with creaturespeakers as with anyone else.

It had been Loulou and Evie's idea to line up a few speakers, to speed up the process of testing his ability. James, however, was not fond of being tested. He decided to change the subject, to focus on Evie for a bit.

"So, you can speak to, er, corvids too?"

"Sure." Evie said. "Corvids, and anything else that flies: birds, bats."

"Insects?" asked James.

Evie rolled her eyes.

"No. Funnily enough. You need to spend a few months with Agent Loulou I reckon. What's Agent Zed think he's doing? No-one can speak to insects, James. Most people can't even speak to anything smaller than a hedgehog. Oh – and no-one does fish. Or anything underwater. I can't *believe* you didn't know that."

James felt angry on Grandad's behalf. He didn't like to hear Evie criticise him. At the same time, however, he wished Grandad *had* told him more about creaturespeak before sending him out here. He heard a polite cough behind him. Loulou had returned, accompanied.

"Hello … boy?" This quiet voice came from a fox, standing a few feet to Loulou's left, having edged out from behind her.

"Hello, er, Mr Fox."

The fox smiled. Well, James thought the fox smiled, its voice certainly did.

"Good to see a proper level of respect in a young human." He was addressing Loulou rather than James. Loulou gestured back at James with her nose and the fox continued. "I gather I am here so you can be certain you can understand me. Given that you already speak to this agent here, I suspect there was little doubt, she and I being somewhat distant cousins. Still."

James had a sudden thought.

"I thought all foxes were Misants?"

The other three froze. Silence fell, for several seconds, broken by Evie's sigh:

"Oh Lord."

"What?" said James, folding his arms across his middle. Agent Loulou answered, but spoke to the fox, not James.

"Renard, please forgive him. As you say, he is a *young* human. And very new to Lifelink."

James felt he had already had enough of meeting other creatures and he had so far only met two. Renard tilted his head to one side, as if considering something.

"I'm not offended. Most speaking foxes *are* probably in that camp. But I, young person, am not. Nor are many others. You cannot judge a fox by its fur. I believe there are in fact more *neutrals* than belong to both organisations. I, however, am a member of Lifelink – just as you are. It's a matter of personal choice you know, not just upbringing."

"I'm sorry," said James, as he felt he should, adding: "Thank you very much, for coming here."

"Ah," Renard was smiling again. "You see. Respect. The knowledge will grow." He turned to head back into the woods, and Agent Loulou thanked him too, before he trotted away.

"So," said Agent Loulou. "I saw you speak to a rook? That's a start. If you can do birds, it's very likely you can also understand bats, and that *would* be useful. I actually can't. I can't do anything rodent, even though I can do feathered flight." It took James a moment to realise that a bat was indeed a rodent.

"I can," Evie smirked. "I can do bats and rats. Almost no-one can speak rat ... Not that it's much use," she added after a moment. "Rats are not at all like the cartoons. They're a bit thick about anything not rat-related. *Their* conversations are about as useful as birds'." James, who had thought the rook had sounded very clever indeed, was confused. Evie could apparently tell from his face. "Well, small birds I mean. Believe me, sparrows are the worst."

"*Anyway* ..." said Agent Loulou. "We can't do otters here ... we'll need a zoo trip for that. Zed said there was a mole who was going to show up but no sign yet. We're also waiting on a hedgehog and a stoat. We couldn't get a weasel, but of course if the stoat turns up then it won't matter."

"They're here," said a muffled voice. James looked round sharply.

"What?" said Loulou.

"Sooo, are you going to? You don't have to … you know," said the voice. James peered downwards under the bench, but saw nothing, no-one.

"James?" snapped Loulou. "What is it?"

"Er, I thought … someone else was here," he said, sounding lame even to himself. All at once, just beside his trainers, there was a ruffling of the grass and bits of soil broke open in a small explosion of turf. James caught a glimpse of claws. He jumped, and moved his feet rapidly away. The other two exchanged a nod.

"Ha." Loulou sniffed. "I believe we have a mole amongst us."

The mole's head emerged, tiny, poking its nose left and right. Its head was attached directly to its body, with no visible neck, and sat between two massively oversized, pink and soil-spattered paws. The mole was sniffing rapidly, it's nose twitching this way and that. James suddenly remembered why they were there.

"Hello there, have you come to talk with me? Did Agent Zed ask you?"

"Ooh good," squeaked the mole. "That was terrifying …. Hang on." The head disappeared again and James heard the same high pitched voice. "It's alright. It's them ... It's all fine. I'll be back soon." And the head re-emerged. "Soo sorry, that was my mate. He worries ... A human who speaks mole? That, I had to come and see."

"Can you?" said James. "See me?"

"James," whispered Evie. "Is the mole speaking to you?"

"Yes!" answered James. "I thought you spoke rodent?"

"*Young man!*" squeaked the mole loudly. "I will thank you to get your families sorted out. I am not a mole *rat*. I am a *true* mole. An insectivore to you humans, and *not* a rodent ... And as for seeing you, perhaps not as you would see, no. But I doo know exactly where you are. Seeing is not all about the eyes … That aside, it is very refreshing to find a creaturespeaker who understands us or - at least - our language. You should soo talk with us more often. You need to learn a bit of mole *lore*, I think…"

"OK," said James. "I'll do that. Thanks, er – " The mole just disappeared, leaving a small pile of soil behind her. James could still hear her voice, gradually fading.

"Ooh, not so bad really. It was too bright though ... The boy? He smelled ... young, but he sounded ... hopeful, I think. Yes ... he sounded curious ..." The voices faded and James realised Agent Loulou had been speaking to him.

" ... neither Agent Evie nor myself. Mole could be useful. Even if we only discovered that much today, I would consider it productive."

James heard Evie complain that she could think of better things to do than wait around seeing who James could talk with. She wasn't at all sure why she was even there. James could have gone to the zoo with his grandparents. She and Loulou were supposed to be chasing down Artemis' attackers, Evie complained, not babysitting.

Her rudeness annoyed James. It wasn't his fault she was there after all: they were all just doing what they'd been asked to do. He turned around angrily.

"Well, I'm *sorry*, but Grand-*Agent Zed* asked us to do this. *I* didn't make you come along!"

"Sorry – *what?*" Evie spluttered.

"It's no use complaining that you don't want to be here, and I am definitely not a baby you have to

– sit on. Why don't you just go and start trying to find whoever hurt Artemis? You don't have to stay *here*."

There was a pause.

"Evie," said Agent Loulou. "*Did* you say you wanted to do that?"

"Not … out loud," Evie said. James realised Evie was staring at him with a sort of horror. James stared back but felt his features slowly imitating Evie's expression.

"*Oh, I* … Oh, I'm *sorry*, I –" James ground to a halt. Then added quietly: "But you did think those things. And it *isn't* my fault."

"No," agreed Agent Loulou. "It isn't."

"I don't want him *reading my mind!*" Evie burst out. She jumped up and took several steps away from the bench. "That is *not* right."

"Don't worry," said Loulou in a low growl. "You were sitting right next to him, thinking about him – and thinking about him somewhat angrily it appears. If you'd been standing over there, or wondering what James had for breakfast, I doubt he would have heard you. If he listened for you in particular, he might have heard something, but it would probably be like static. He wouldn't have a focus. He needs a *reason* to pick something up."

James didn't think Evie looked any less horrified.

"But I hear Mr T all the time!" he said.

"No, you don't," said Loulou. "You hear Mr T a lot of the time. You don't hear him when he focuses on you *not* hearing him, you don't hear him when he's not nearby, you don't hear him when his thoughts have nothing to do with you – there are a lot of times you don't hear Mr T. If you heard him 'all the time' he'd be a constant voice in your head." James studied the ground, realising the truth of what Loulou was saying. "You have conversations with Mr T when he directly speaks to you, or when he directly thinks about you. If you tried, you could probably pick him up on other occasions, but you might not be able to understand him. And if he knew you were listening and didn't want you to understand, then you wouldn't. Sub-verbal creaturespeak is not telepathy as you think of it. But it *is* useful …" Loulou fell quiet for a moment. "It is incredibly useful. And your skills are growing apace young man. I think we'll call it a day and head on back to Ops – I can't see that hedgehog, or stoat, turning up now – and, I need to see your Grandad."

Loulou strode off, and James hurried to catch up, so he could talk to her and ask how exactly it could be 'useful'.

James was dimly aware that Evie was trailing behind them, keeping her distance.

CHAPTER 21

SEARCHING FOR MISANTS

Tᴵᴛᴀɴ ʜᴀᴅ ᴏɴʟʏ ever known the man before him as the Stranger. When the human had first wandered into their midst that had been what people called him and – whatever his original name – he now answered to that.

The Stranger was, in many ways, the ideal human. He lived in the woodland, in shelter he had himself constructed, he hunted and fished. Although he used fire, he used it only for cooking. For warmth he used woollen coverings and to strengthen his feet he wore leather. Titan could condone the Stranger's lifestyle, but what was *useful* was that this same man had huge knowledge of the other humans' world. He was a source of vast information. The two had had some very frank discussions and Titan understood that this man thought, in many ways, as he did. Despite being human, he recognised that mankind had devasted the Earth and he was intent on making amends. The man's latest suggestion had been most interesting. The Stranger had explained, at great length, how Misant action taken against just a few men could affect human plans deeply.

Titan was interested in the men involved in creating destructive machinery. He and the Stranger were even now refining plans they had made for the attack. If successful, it would give new hope to Misants - in England, but also in countries all over the world. Titan could hardly believe such an opportunity had fallen into his claws. Neither he, nor the human, could pull it off alone – but if animals and the Stranger worked together, then it was entirely possible.

Titan had sent word to several Misant cells and a number of operatives were already mobilised, ordered to move at the Stranger's command.

Agent Michiko passed the receiver to Ash, who spoke into it rapidly.

"It's Agent Sheera we've got to thank. She's been out over the locality for days now, since the first whispers, just trying to spot anything a bit odd. That's how she found the man with the hawk. Some kind of weird Pagan healer – Lifelinker - found the hawk half dead and took it home. It can't fly now though. It just lives with the healer –"

"Could you possibly get on with it, agent?" Singh's voice was loud enough for Michiko to hear too.

"Yeah, sorry, course. Well – anyway, the point was – it couldn't fly cos it had been mauled, badly, by this badger called Titan. I remembered your comms about Agent Artemis and realised we needed that hawk's information. But it was Sheera got her to talk, and – guess what?" This last fell into silence. "Oh, well – the hawk used to be a Misant operative – but, not only that, she was actually one of the Harris hawks that attacked *Agent Artemis!* What are the odds, eh? But, and here's the thing –"

"*Yes?*" said Agent Singh.

"This Titan is working with a *human*. The hawk – her name's Kiya by the way – didn't know what the guy was called. They all just know him as '*the Stranger*'. She couldn't tell me much about him – she said he had 'autumn coloured' hair." Ash chuckled. "But they don't really notice people same as we do. Anyway, apparently he's been around for *years*, but lately he's become Titan's best friend. I reckon we need to find out who this *Stranger* is." Ash stopped speaking, but he was nodding his head in agreement with himself.

"Yes, Agent Ash. Indeed we do … And *have* you?

"Well, er, no. We came straight back to report. Whoever he is, he'll be in hiding, so it'll be quite difficult to locate him I expect ..." Ash trailed off.

"No doubt. Make that your top priority. Oh – and tell Agent Sheera her information is very much appreciated. Keep her out there, will you?"

"Yes, sir." Ash replied as he ended the call, replacing the Ops phone on the desk. "Did you get that, then?"

Ash was addressing a large raven perched silently on the back of the desk chair, her head hunched into her shoulders, waiting.

"Yehhs." Sheera croaked, adding: "I will stohp for food firrst." She stretched her wings, flapping them twice and creating a breeze. "And short sleeep. Does he noht know how lonng, flyying?"

"No he does not," Michiko said. "And I suspect he does not greatly care. He's as worried as we are. We should start getting some support by morning. Ash, you guys take five then, and I'll check on supplies.

Trouble is I'm not sure who we're getting yet. Human, feather or canine presumably." She sighed. "I'll get Ops ready for a meeting."

Ash raised his hand in a salute as he headed for the door. There was a swoosh as the large black bird looped down from the chair, closing her wings to slide on through the doorway after her colleague. Michiko linked her hands behind her back and pushed them down until her shoulders cracked, twice, then headed for Ops.

"OK, *Stranger*," she said aloud, to no-one. "Let's hunt you down."

When James and his companions arrived back at Ops South, all the adults and cats were there, but no-one was speaking to each other and James felt awkward for no reason the moment he entered. Agent Loulou cut though the silence.

"What's happened?"

She addressed Grandma. Grandad had his back to them all, tapping away at the Ops computer. Mum was sitting on the couch, tight-lipped. Artemis and Mr T sat side by side on the table. James watched them turning their heads at exactly the same time to look first at Agent Loulou, then to Grandma, as each one spoke.

"It's Agent Singh," Grandma said.

"It is *not!*" Mum suddenly shouted up. James guessed she realised Grandma was answering Loulou. "Or it wouldn't be, if *you* hadn't notified him." Mum fell silent. Grandma tried again.

"Yes. Well, we informed Agent Singh of James' apparent similarity to his father ... Er, how did it go today, Lou, by the way?"

James saw Mum shoot Agent Loulou a razor-like stare. Loulou talked in a low rumble while Mum just frowned.

"It went well. He spoke to a few but, more importantly, he *heard* Evie – and a mole we think – *sub*-verbally. Seems like he's developing fast, so we can probably expect a lot more."

James, who was proud that he had done well, beamed at Grandma despite feeling something like electricity in the atmosphere. Then he realised, abruptly, that Mum required translation.

"I spoke to more animals, Mum."

"That's super, James," Grandma said, but then added: "Though also problematic. Helen?" Mum looked quickly from agent to agent and, when she spoke, her voice sounded … uncertain. Which was not at all like Mum.

"It appears that, there is some big Misant – thing – going on, most likely in Gloucestershire, and they need to know *what*. And, apparently, the easiest way for them to find out, currently – is by transporting a *twelve-year-old* to the vicinity, so he can - listen in." James wasn't sure if Mum was angry or frightened, but she was something alright.

"Mum, I don't mind!" James said. "I'd like to help. It's just listening, and telling people what was said, right? I can do that ... Well, I'm pretty sure I can do that …" he finished a little weakly, realising that none of them was yet sure what he could, or couldn't, do.

Grandma grinned warmly.

"That's good of you, dear, but it depends on whether or not your Mum thinks it's for the best."

Mum's shoulders sagged, as if someone had dropped the strings that held her upright. There was complete quiet for a moment, until she spoke. Her voice was very calm now but, oddly James thought, she was staring at Grandma – even though she was talking to him.

"Of course you may go, James. If there is really *no other* way – and your grandparents have convinced me there is *not* – then you have to help. But you must check in with me here every day and – agents," Mum scanned the whole room fiercely, "you *need* to promise me that my son's welfare comes before *anything* else. Is that something you can do?"

Agent Loulou spoke up.

"I will take full responsibility. I will ensure there is someone with him at all times and that he is kept safe."

Grandma translated and James thought Mum looked slightly more accepting of the situation. Just slightly. Loulou spoke again.

"Evie, I think she might be happier if her son were with someone to whom Helen could also speak. It strikes me that it would be a good idea if you were to take James under your wing, so to speak, and perhaps play a similar role to the one I took with you?"

James saw Evie's eyes open enormously wide in an expression that could only be described as horrified. Evie spoke in a whisper.

"Mrs Doughty, Agent Loulou just suggested that I mentor James during the trip, but I realise you would probably want someone a bit older, more resp –"

"No! I wouldn't!" Mum jumped up. "That's a *good* idea! Agent Loulou will still be in charge, won't she?" Evie nodded. "So *she's* the one responsible anyway, but I think learning from you would really suit James. You were a newcomer not so long ago, and you don't have all that Lifelink … baggage. And you're someone else who can talk to Agent Loulou for me. I'd be very OK with that … James?"

James was glad to agree to anything that allowed him to go on his first Lifelink adventure, so he just nodded happily.

"Right then," Grandma said. "Looks like some of us are headed out on a trip."

"*Em!*" Grandad's voice cut through the conversation. "Come here. Read this." It was said so sharply that James, and everyone in the room, stopped still and waited.

Grandma did as she was asked, reaching out to clutch Grandad's forearm for just a second when they both turned around to face the room. Grandad started to speak to everyone and James watched Grandma move quietly over to sit beside Mum.

"It's a communiqué from HQ. Actually it's sent *Covering Secret* from Agent Singh. They have some information, from Ops West." Grandad's eyebrows were knotted together fearsomely. "The Misants there are working with a human who is high up in their ranks. It's been confirmed. Ops West have been trying to find out what they can, but all they know is this. He's known by Misants as 'the *Stranger*' and has been rising through their ranks for what seems to be - the last six or seven years." He stopped, cleared his throat, then continued. "Before that, well, before that it seems it's as if he didn't exist - there are no stories, nothing. But he speaks with everything. Everything. He is Titan's right-hand man, literally. No-one … no-one knows where he came from –" Grandad's features were skewed into a deep frown.

"It's mis-information," said Mr T, at the same time as Mum said:

"What are you saying, Zedekiah?"

James was confused. He concentrated hard on Mr T and thought:

I don't understand!

Mr T jumped, very slightly, but replied calmly:

It's a Misant rumour James. They are trying to undermine us, but it won't work.

What do you mean? James replied. Mr T hesitated. Then:

It's the same sort of time that your Dad went missing. It's a dirty trick, James. They are trying to cast doubt into our minds and we mustn't let it work.

James knew no-one else had heard Mr T, so shouted up over the discussion, interrupting all the adults:

"Is my *Dad* alive?" Even as he said it, and the group fell quiet, the meaning of the discussion hit him, hard. "Is my – *Dad* … a *Misant?*"

CHAPTER 22

ADVENTURERS

EVIE KNEW SHE had changed considerably over the last few weeks. She was no longer thrown when addressed by passing creatures and had easily accepted being a member of a secret organisation. She had begun to feel very at home – for the first time in her life – and had developed a real bond with Loulou. She imagined this was what it was like to have an aunt, or a much older sister, who knew all the things Evie didn't yet. Evie felt like she had family now and was more comfortable in the Lifelink world than she had ever dreamed possible. Until the boy had read her thoughts.

Evie now steadfastly chose not to talk with the child in that way. Or talk to him much at all if she could help it. Evie admitted to herself, she had been creeped out by the experience, the sheer weirdness of knowing someone was looking at your thoughts. It was just plain *wrong* to have someone else reach into your brain. She guessed she wouldn't have minded so much if it had been Loulou, but there was no-one else on the planet she wanted to share any of her thoughts.

Evie was already feeling uneasy when they got the news about the 'Stranger' – who seemed to be related to the Doughty family – and that got everyone *else* spooked too. Evie was now keener than ever to get off on the mission and solve the mystery that had everyone so upset. She was informed by Agent Zed, however, that they were expecting an operative from thirty miles away to come and drive them up to Gloucestershire. Evie consoled herself with the thought that at least they would be travelling comfortably this time. Agent Zed had another surprise too though.

"We'll be needing this evening for a bit of training before you leave."

He had carried on ticking off his nightly checks on all the operatives' signals and Evie had had to ask:

"Sorry …? Training who? James?"

"No, no my dear." Agent Zed clicked the final window closed and turned around smiling broadly. "Your training! We need to get you up to speed. Well, maybe not up to speed, but good for something anyway."

Evie was speechless. Good for *something?* She heard Agent Zed chuckle.

"Combat, Agent Evie, good for combat."

Evie was stumped. Combat? What on Earth was the old guy on about now? Zed's grin dropped and was replaced with a very level gaze that got her attention.

"Young lady, it obviously hasn't yet either crossed your mind or been explained to you – but, as an agent working for Lifelink, you may find yourself in situations that are somewhat … difficult. Misant operatives are not generally well disposed towards us, as Artemis over there will doubtless confirm."

"They had me out-numbered," Artemis hissed from her spot on the green cushion. "I can be pretty unfriendly myself."

"I don't doubt it, agent, not for a moment. Anyway," Zed continued, "you may find yourself in a situation where you need to defend yourself – or indeed my grandson – physically."

So, Evie mused, now she was a bodyguard as well as a babysitter.

"OK," she said. "I'm pretty fit you know. I did a bit of self-defence last year actually – karate. I thought we were leaving tomorrow though? How are you going to find someone to train me in anything before then?"

Evie noticed the corner of Zed's mouth twitch.

"Luckily for you, your trainer's already here." He performed a small bow and a flourish with one arm.

"You?" Evie was shocked. Then, realising she had been rude: "I mean. No offence, but, well – aren't you a bit too … too senior, these days?" She finished, hearing herself sound just as awkward as she now felt.

"Old? Yes I'm old enough. So old I've done quite of few of these missions myself and tried out the techniques I'm going to show you for real. In the heat of the moment and all that. You'll find Loulou - who, I might add, is getting on a bit herself these days – has a few advantages you don't. Mostly, they're teeth."

Evie could see the truth of that and found she was starting to wonder seriously about how dangerous this Lifelink job would turn out to be.

"I reckon I could put up a pretty good fight if someone did attack me," she said. "I do remember the classes."

"Good," said Zed. "That'll help. Now what if that someone who attacks you is, say, a Rottweiler?" Evie blinked. It was a perfectly reasonable question she realised. Zed carried on. "No, I don't suppose they covered that in karate. Don't worry. Two things. One, you'll be with Loulou - who will try to avoid any situation that could possibly lead to confrontation and – two, if there is any confrontation she will be at the forefront of it, with you standing firmly behind and well back. Hopefully steering my grandson to somewhere safe in fact. But," and here he paused, observing her steadily. "If things go wrong at any point, you need to at the very least be able to get away. So, this is a short, but very serious class. OK?" Evie nodded. He definitely had her attention now.

"OK," Zed stood up, hands on hips, and surveyed her. "This is pretty obvious, but if you are facing a dog - or even a badger - it is an unfair match. You have no weapons and probably less strength. The first thing you try to do is even that up. You need a weapon, if you can. British Citizens don't carry firearms of course and, anyhow, if we could so could the human Misants. You need to find a club, an object, something you can wield – anything, from a walking stick to a bicycle pump. Or something hard like a brick. Also, if there is higher ground, that's where you want to be – make them work to reach you. Stand on something, run up steps, get further uphill. All you're aiming to do is injure. You need to buy time so you can get away. Got that?" Evie found she was concentrating hard on everything Zed said now, repeating it inside her head, remembering it.

"Yes."

"Right. I am going to show you how to use your body weight to the best effect, and the spots to attack that give you the best chance of running, starting with the eye sockets. But for that, I shall need my able assistant. I believe she is waiting for us in the back garden ..."

Nearly two hours later, Evie tottered back into the house and collapsed, heaving for breath, into one of the living room armchairs. She was followed by Agent Zed, who strode in breathing deeply and evenly, then Loulou who padded in behind them both and headed over to the water bowl, lapping rhythmically.

"Thanks Lou," Zed said. "It's a while since I've had do a demonstration, reckon I'm a bit rusty."

"Rusty?" sobbed Evie. "You are joking, right?"

"Actually, he's not," huffed Loulou, giving herself a shake to loosen up. "Back in the day, eh, Zed?"

Zed smiled, lips pressed tight.

"Yes, back in the day, I'd have run rings round you girl. I guess we're both a bit older and wiser now."

Evie was hanging her head, looking despondently at the carpet as she waited for her heart rate to return to normal.

"Hey, you did really well, Evie," Agent Zed said. "You're quicker than most on your first lesson. Just keep practising." He lowered his voice to a whisper. "You're quicker than Em was when we started out!"

"I am not so old I'm *deaf* you know!" Evie heard an indignant voice from the kitchen, then Agent Em popped her head through the doorway. "But … if what Zed says is correct, then you should be proud. Loulou will carry on getting you up to speed. You can have a practise session like that one every day!"

"Oh, great," breathed Evie. "Great."

The next morning James was awake at six. Mum met him with a bright smile and scrambled eggs on toast.

"Eat it all up - it'll keep you going. Off to Ops in an hour or so!"

James tucked in while Mum, unusually, sat down opposite him with a cup of tea, watching him eat. She chatted with him about the journey, guessing how long it might take and what he might see on the way. James did notice however that, despite talking continuously, Mum did not once mention the man they were now all calling 'the Stranger.'

This seemed odd because the only thing James had been able to think about since yesterday was the report of the Stranger. Mr T had continued to explain it as either a coincidence or deliberate Misant misinformation. James couldn't work out whether Mr T actually believed that or whether he was trying to make James feel better. Being able to communicate sub-verbally did not seem to help at all with whether or not the speaker was being honest, which was disappointing.

James himself was not sure what he wished. Since his Dad's disappearance, they had never admitted to more than the fact that 'the worst' *could* have happened. Until they knew for sure, how could they? But if he had been alive, they could think of no reason why he wouldn't have contacted them. So, in his heart of hearts, James had believed for years that his Dad had to be gone from the world. The possibility that he might still be alive had been amazing for a moment, but then immediately awful at the same time. First, it was just a suggestion with no evidence to back it up. But second, if this person *was* James' Dad, then something must have gone terribly wrong. *How* could he have left his family behind, and become a leader of *Misants?*

James discovered that this new knowledge felt almost worse than all the years without even a clue. Last night, Mum had agreed with Mr T although, again, James was not sure she meant it. In the end, everyone said that there was no point whatsoever in guessing until they knew something more.

The possibilities sat curled up inside James now, like a heavy marble of worry rolling around and making him feel odd. He did his best to ignore it and pinned a cheerful expression to his face. He didn't want to worry Mum. So, they both chatted away on the drive to Grandma's, without James saying a word of what was really on his mind.

The transport to Gloucestershire was not quite what James had expected. It turned out to be an old, red ex-Post Office van, with six seats and plenty of parcel space. Evie and James sat in the second row with their backpacks stowed between their feet. Artemis, who was finally heading back out into the field, was being given a ride nearer to her home base and was resting on a blanket in the middle seat. James had been amazed to discover that Artemis lived most of the time with an old lady, a non-speaker, who - Artemis reminded Grandad - would by now have noticed her unusually long absence, despite the half dozen or so other cats she housed.

Loulou sat upfront along with their driver and Gizmo – who was a Jack Russell terrier. The driver was a Lifelink operative (though not an agent) who went by the name of 'Rags', which James found confusing. He kept mixing up the names of the two newcomers in his head. Rags was tall and skinny, wearing oil-stained jeans, and an old, grey T-shirt bearing the faded words *AceOfSpades*. His mousy hair was in need of a cut, James decided, and was held back from his face by a grimy, red sweatband.

Despite this, Rags seemed to take natural command of the little group from the start – telling them where to sit, checking they had remembered all their bags, and putting the address into the satnav. He then made sure the human passengers and Loulou were all fastened into their seatbelts. Loulou sniffed a little, saying it was quite unnecessary, but a confident grin from Rags seemed to convince her that they weren't setting off before she agreed to be buckled in. Gizmo was lying in a rather high-sided, cushioned dog-basket, on the floor in front of the passenger seat – so James could hear him occasionally but not see him.

They had been travelling for a few miles, and the traffic was beginning to thin out, when Loulou seemed to decide that the journey would pass more quickly with a little conversation. Until then apart from the rattling of the van itself, it had been completely quiet once they had set off, with each passenger deep in thought about where they were heading, and Rags concentrating on traffic.

"So," said Loulou. "I knew another *Rags* a few years back. He's retired now – gone to live in Dorset. He got his name as a puppy of course, because he used to chew everything to pieces. Don't suppose that's how you got yours?" The human Rags burst out laughing, so loudly he startled the other passengers, then he slapped the steering wheel with the flat of his right hand.

"Oh I *like* you Agent Loulou! Better than some of the stiffs I get to transport. You can barely pry a conversation out of half of them, much less find a sense of humour." Rags seemed to remember the question and added: "It's short for *Oily Rag* actually. I'm a mechanic by trade. You can maybe tell?"

James, who had imagined the name was a reference to their driver's clothes, couldn't stop himself saying: 'Ohh' – as in 'oh, I get it now' – which caused Rags to glance at him in the rear view mirror and once more reveal a mouthful of formidable teeth.

"I'm guessing *you* thought it was because I was a bit of a hobo?" James' stomach felt as if it was dissolving with his embarrassment, but Rags did not seem in the least bit offended. Loulou ignored them and said:

"That's useful. I assume you don't just do cars?"

"Nope. I can fix pretty much anything, though I say so myself. Come in handy a few times when you agents've needed something – well, not so much fixing as *un*-fixing, if you get my drift." James could tell from his voice that Rags enjoyed, and was proud of, his work.

"We are certainly glad to have you with us, Rags," said Loulou. "Do you have another assignment after delivering us?"

"Not directly, no."

"Well, if you fancy sticking around for a while we might have some use for your particular skills. No promises, mind, we're not exactly sure what we're going there to do yet. But if you're at a loose end …"

"What d'you reckon, Gizmo?" Rags winked at his invisible friend. James heard a muffled voice respond:

"With you, mate. As ever."

CHAPTER 23

OPS WEST

WHEN ASH CAME back from his latest ear-to-the-ground mission – and, in Sheera's case, the air – he was greeted by the sight of Michiko hunched over her desk. She was thumbing through hard copy printouts, glancing up at first one screen on her desk, then the other, and muttering constantly:

"*What's* your target, what *is* your target?"

Every few seconds she would run a hand through her bobbed hair, with the result that it now stayed sticking out at a number of angles, giving her the appearance of a mad professor.

"No luck, then, Mitch?" Michiko spared him a brief glance, face hidden under beetled brows with her head still down. "Well, maybe this'll help. There's something to do with a plane. Sheera spotted an unusual group near the town centre, at the back of the box warehouse? Homeless guy, by appearance anyway, but with a cat – not a dog – and a couple of crows nearby, not flying off, just staying there despite the company. So, I got pretty close to them and caught the tail end of the conversation before something spooked one of the birds." Ash paused, but Michiko just watched him until he continued. "They were speakers sure enough and they were estimating how long it might take 'the target' to get 'there from the airport.' I'm not sure they ever said where 'there' was, sorry. Or, if they did I didn't catch it, but it's something at least. Can you use it?"

Michiko breathed out. She seemed to be quietly counting as she did. Then she spoke, softly, through lips that barely moved: "So, how long?" Ash looked confused. "How long did they think it would take to get 'there' from the airport?"

"Oh, *right* – didn't I say?" Ash grinned. "Sorry! Well, they argued about it a bit, to be honest. The guy thought about half an hour to forty minutes, the birds less. The guy said a vehicle couldn't travel that fast in traffic and that the birds only did distance 'as the crow flies' so how could they know? Then the cat weighed in and said he'd heard his humans saying they needed to allow twice as long if they were going to the airport, because of all the traffic, so maybe they should take that into account too, so –" Michiko's head was now wedged firmly, face-down, onto the palms of her hands. Ash suddenly noticed this. "Mitch?"

"Ash. So – are we going with half an hour then?"

"Um, yes. We're going with the guy, because like I said, he's probably not your regular homeless guy at all. Do you want me to stay and give you a hand here for a bit now?"

"No!" Michiko's head popped back up. "I'm fine. That's some useful information. You, er, carry on."

"OK, laters." Ash breezed out of the room as if he hadn't a care in the world.

Michiko sighed deeply, then clicked back on one of the maps, positioned the cursor over the airport and dragged a red circle outwards to a distance of about twenty miles, before clicking 'enlarge'.

"Right," she said. "*Where's* your target, where *is* your target?" She pushed her fingers backwards through her fringe.

James and his companions arrived at their destination that afternoon – all except Artemis, who had hopped out near her home, slipping over a wall and vanishing. The Post Office van pulled up outside a stone cottage, set back from the side of the road, with a wide gravel driveway. James caught sight of a couple of outbuildings behind the cottage and noticed the garden was mostly weeds. He also saw a pick-up truck, parked in the garden, and an old mini around to the side. The cottage was surrounded by fields, but James had read the road sign they had just passed, which said two miles to Rodmarton – presumably the nearest town.

James had fallen asleep somewhere along the M4 and not woken up until they had left the motorway far behind. He had seen a few houses, more fields – with cows and sometimes sheep, dotted about. It had been spitting with rain when he fell asleep and now the sky was the colour of steel, so James zipped up his hoodie and folded his arms for warmth.

"Here we are then!" Rags shouted into the back, which ensured James was properly awake. "Everyone out!"

They all followed orders then began stretching and stamping their feet noisily on the gravel, before huddling around the doorway to the cottage as Rags rang the bell. The door was opened by a woman, maybe as old as Mum, but dressed in jeans and a sweatshirt, with crazily punky hair. She gestured for them to come inside, then closed the door behind them. They all stood awkwardly in a line in the hallway.

"Hello! Welcome. Sorry it's such a miserable day." The woman greeted them while she scanned the group and settled her gaze on Agent Loulou.

"Agent Loulou – from HQ? Delighted to see *you*. I'm Agent Michiko, as you doubtless know. Agents Ash and Sheera are out gathering intel, but they'll be here later. You'll meet them at supper." She turned towards Rags, lifting her eyebrows as a question.

"Hi – I'm Rags. Don't you worry about me agent, I'm just the driver. Gizmo and me can easy kip in the van. I'm just hanging on for a bit, in case Agent Loulou here needs me."

"Right you are," said Agent Michiko. "But we have plenty of room here. There are some dorms out the back – bunk beds, bathrooms. Just across the yard. We act as a half-way house for defectors." James stared, but Michiko carried on with no change in her no-nonsense voice. "There are rooms to suit human needs and others with different sleeping arrangements – they're all clean." As she spoke, she lifted a key from a hook near the front door and passed it to Rags. "We're eating at seven."

Rags, clearly dismissed, slipped back out of the house with Gizmo at his heels.

"Right …" said Michiko. "Follow me, please."

James followed the others, who entered the next doorway along, which led to a large and comfortable room. There were a couple of desks with computers, a filing cabinet and cupboards; but also, big squashy sofas, thick rugs and a fireplace with a fake 'real' fire glowing cheerfully. Michiko strode over to one of the desks and stood behind it, waving her hands about to tell the others to make themselves at home.

"Thank you," said Loulou. "I need to introduce you to Probationary Agent Evie." Evie gave Michiko a small smile and perched on the arm of a sofa. "And the young gentleman here is James. Jake Doughty's son." Michiko looked up sharply.

"Probationary Agent Evie." She nodded at Evie, then studied James for a long second or two before saying:

"Is he … working with you?"

"I know," Loulou agreed. "He's a little young for this type of thing, but we think he can speak to a lot of different species and we're hoping he might be able to help us pinpoint the target, if we can get him near the right people. Which would be where you came in of course."

"Quite," Michiko said. James felt a bubble of pride rise in his chest as he realised the agent had just accepted him as part of the task force. "Agent Ash is out hoping to locate the Misant cell now. We want to follow one of their operatives, until we find a group, then get someone with the right ear to listen in. At least that's our best bet at the moment. We have some intel and I have been trying to locate a probable target within this area." Michiko swung the screen round to show everyone the map. As she did so, she lifted her face up, and seemed to see them all properly for the first time.

"Agents, forgive me, would you like to sort yourselves out a room each first, and come back here when you've had time to recover from the journey? Just take one of the keys from the hallway."

With muttered 'thank yous', they did as suggested, Evie grabbing a key and Loulou leading the way round to the buildings at the back. The key had a green fob and it turned out to very sensibly open the door of the same colour. As they went in, James could see Rags and Gizmo striding across one of the fields nearby, stretching their long and short legs.

The rooms were warm and basic. James and Evie slung their backpacks onto bunks in the two bedrooms and Loulou pushed open the doors to the two other rooms. One was a bathroom. The other was a large room obviously intended for non-human occupancy, with some comfortable bedding across one corner and a door that, like the front door, swung open when pushed from either direction.

"Ah, this will do nicely!" Loulou said. "Right, Evie. You should be ready for a bit of exercise after that journey. I know I am. We'll take up where we left off with the lessons. James – have you checked the signal for your tablet?" James assured her he had, and that it was working. He was in fact already signing on to CollegeLine and logging into his classroom. He had an hour's session due to start. It seemed crazy to James that he could be out here at the start of a mission with Lifelink agents, yet still be required to sign in for school at the scheduled time. Loulou had been very clear, however, on the fact that she understood the need for a human education and that James could log in from the middle of a field if need be. James had moodily agreed. He also quickly messaged Mum to assure her all was well.

A couple of hours later, the little group rejoined Agent Michiko to meet agents Sheera and Ash. They all gathered in the large kitchen, where Michiko and Ash provided Loulou and Gizmo with a stewed beef supper, then removed three huge pizzas from a big oven for the humans, which they ate with salad and cans of diet coke while they talked around the table.

The evening turned out to be very pleasant, a bit like a party, with no mention of the work they were to begin tomorrow. Rags seemed at home in any company and, to James' delight, he even had Agent Michiko laughing. Agent Ash was as chatty as Rags, and James found himself laughing along with his new friends and glad that he was a part of the group. Agent Sheera was as quiet as Ash was noisy, though. She perched on what looked like a purpose-made bar, which had a beanbag next to it. James was sitting at the table, but he noticed Evie wander over to the beanbag and lower herself down with her head against the wall, chatting quietly with the raven. James assumed she was simply sitting as far away from him as she could. Sheera, however, left when they sat down to eat – so Evie squeezed a stool in between Michiko and Rags at the other end of the room. Ash explained that Sheera hunted for her own food and, as he told James, she did not visit Ops every day. Ash said he and the raven had been working together on and off for over two years. She was the eyes of Lifelink for an area of about fifty miles of the Gloucestershire countryside. If anyone could find the Misant cell, Ash told James, he had no doubt that Sheera would.

That night, after supper, James found it strange settling down in the stiff sheets and heavy blankets of his bunk, without Mum or Grandma saying goodnight. James left his door ajar for the light and was just drifting off, when he noticed a large, Loulou-shaped shadow padding towards him.

"I just came to say 'goodnight', James," Loulou said. "And to check that you're OK?" James snuggled down, feeling more cosy, and told Agent Loulou he was looking forward to tomorrow. "Good boy," Loulou whispered, in low woof, giving his arm a friendly nudge before backing softly out of the room.

CHAPTER 24

CONTACT

IN THE MORNING, James found his way back to the kitchen, where the others were already gathered – helping themselves to toast, cereal, fruit and chicken chunks in gravy. James sat in a spare seat next to Ash and organised some toast and a glass of orange juice for himself, while listening in on the conversations around him. The adults seemed to have been up for a while.

Through the window, James could see a large black bird, clearly Sheera, tearing something apart on the lawn before flying up to the trees. He turned away to look at the others. Agent Michiko was mid-sentence.

"… the best news we've had in ages Ash. I say a group of us goes over there this morning in case there's anything more to find. Agent, maybe you could lead on that?"

She meant Loulou, who paused to nod, before heading over to a dish of water to round off her breakfast. James looked around the table, hoping someone would notice him. Rags did.

"It's good news lad, we're off on another little trip. Your people here have found the Misant base, or so they think. Place called Badgers Copse. I'll drive you there. We can get within about a quarter of a mile by road. You up for that Gizmo?" The little terrier was curled up on a rug, contentedly digesting his chicken.

"No problem," Gizmo responded, stretching his short legs till they shook, before jumping to his feet. "Could do with a run."

"Are you coming, Ash?" James asked. Ash looked over at Michiko.

"No, I don't think so." The senior agent answered for him. "Agents Evie, Loulou and yourself should suffice. We don't want to go tramping in there with an army. This is more of a covert trip."

An hour later they pulled into a lay-by off a country lane. Just across a field there were a few trees, like a small wood, and Rags said that that was where they were headed.

"Gizmo and me'll wait here," he said. "We won't go far so if you need a quick get-away we'll see you coming!" He laughed as he leaned across and shoved the passenger door open for Loulou to jump out. Evie, Loulou and James then hopped over – or through – a stile, into the field, and began trudging across the rough grass towards the trees.

"So," Evie broke their silence. "What are we hoping to find, Loulou?"

"I'm not sure," Loulou said, "but this is the place that's been mentioned on the grapevine more than any other. It's a place to start."

"Weird kind of headquarters," James said. Evie placed her hands on her hips and studied James as they walked.

"Not so weird if your leader's – say – a badger though, maybe?"

"Oh. Yeah." James felt a familiar warming of his neck, as he often did when Evie spoke to him. They covered the rest of the distance in silence until they were within a few metres of the trees. Loulou spoke to them, under her panting breath.

"We'll just go to the middle of the copse and wait a while. I'll have a scout round, see what I can find. Evie, you watch out for any movement. We can see what sorts of creatures hang around here. If they have a hawk, we've probably already been spotted, so just act like you're a brother and sister out walking your dog."

James and Evie exchanged a startled glance. Evie's mouth twitched and she bent down and picked up a stick, throwing it as hard as she could towards the trees.

"Fetch!" She called. Loulou paused for a second, locking eyes with Evie, then suddenly bounded off and disappeared into the bracken at the edge of the copse. James giggled and hurried to catch up with Evie as she followed Loulou. They entered the trees to see Loulou waiting with the stick held in her teeth. As Evie drew near, Loulou dropped the stick and turned to head further into the trees.

"Good *girl!*" Evie called. Loulou did not respond, though it seemed to James her back stiffened a little as she walked on ahead. After a minute or two they came into a small clearing with a fallen tree. Evie hopped up onto the makeshift seat and James leaned up against the opposite end near the roots. Loulou sniffed her way around, through the grass and bracken, scrabbling at bits of twigs and following different scents as any dog does. Evie spoke, a little loudly.

"Let's stop here for a few minutes, Ja-ay-son, um, my legs are aching."

"Sure … sis." James replied, feeling silly. Evie lay back on her elbows and stretched out. James realised she had given herself a good view of the treetops and sky. He glanced up, thinking of hawks and Artemis. James jumped a little as he heard Loulou's voice in his mind:

James I want you to stay there and just listen. See if you can hear anything.

Loulou herself was still snuffling through the undergrowth, and James understood that, as she was not speaking out loud, neither should he.

I'll try, Agent Loulou, he said doubtfully. *But I'm not sure it works like that. I mean, I need someone to talk to really.*

Just try, even if nothing happens.

James wasn't sure what Loulou was expecting him to hear and was even less sure he could do it. He slid down the tree trunk, folding his knees up, and sat on the scrubby turf using the trunk as a backrest. Then he let his eyelids fall, in the hope he might be able to focus more on hearing. James concentrated on the rustlings of leaves and of small things ticking away in the greenery. He could hear birds chirruping in the branches and his own breath shushing in and out slowly as he tried to relax. He found at first that he was just listening to his breathing, but then he found his thoughts moving into the air around him, as it jostled the small branches near the tops of the trees. It was very soothing and he let his mind wander more. He was imagining being among those twigs, swaying in the breeze – when a single sentence popped into his head speaking in a small voice as if from a great distance:

People! Doing what?

James had an urge to answer but shut down his own inner voice, panicked that he would give them away. At the same time Evie spoke out loud.

"Hey, bro, there's a hawk up there. It's cool."

Then Loulou was speaking inside his head again.

It's probably a lookout but it won't know we are speakers. We don't want to leave as soon as it arrives. That would arouse suspicion. And we haven't finished checking the place out anyway.

James took Loulou's hint and called up to Evie.

"Riight. Cool ... Let's hang around here for a bit. I think ... Daisy's happy, sniffing around." Evie started to say something, stopped, then said:

"Oh! *Right*." She slid down off the tree trunk and mooched around the clearing, bending down and picking up a chunk of branch, weighing it from hand to hand. She did not throw it this time, but held onto it firmly, as she wandered around the edges.

James allowed his eyes to close once more and breathed slowly again, trying to ignore the sounds of Evie's footsteps and Loulou's rustling, listening for the noises that were not theirs.

Evie kicked a tree root. James heard the 'thunk,' and Evie's tutting, and imagined he could feel the vibration of the root where it burrowed into the ground. He created an image of it in his mind, splitting into little branches of roots, then tiny tendrils that carried the vibration of Evie's kick travelling downwards like electricity, deep into the soil.

What was that?

A deep, muffled whisper James felt more than he heard. He shivered and held his breath. The voice continued.

"Brack, are you awake?"

"Yes, sir." Not quite so deep, another voice.

"Get up there and reconnoitre the copse."

"Yes, sir."

James was about to call Loulou when a thought struck him. If he could hear these voices, could they hear him? If he spoke to Loulou would they hear too? He had no idea. There was no reaction to what he was thinking now, so presumably they couldn't hear his private thoughts at least. James was in an agony over what to do, his stomach in knots, when he became aware of a scrabbling noise to his right and a snout pushed its way through a curtain of root debris, just behind the fallen tree. James jumped up, watching the snout, thinking hard.

"Sis," he called over to Evie, who turned towards him. "I think I just saw a badger!"

Before Evie could respond, there was a rough, squawking call from overhead:

"Brack? Stand down? Non-speaking."

At the same time, Loulou trotted over towards them. Then, in a flash, she barrelled towards the tree-trunk base, barking and growling like a mad thing. The snout retreated immediately but Loulou scrabbled at the entrance, growling even louder. James, like Evie, found himself glued to the spot in amazement. Evie was first to react, shaking her head as if waking up.

"Ah … Daisy! Daisy, come here girl. It's just a badger. Leave it." Loulou promptly about-turned and padded obediently back to them. James heard the voices once more.

"Brack? Report!"

"Non-speakers, sir. The dog went after me, but it was too big for the sett. Ny's up on watch."

"Hmm." The owner of the deep voice was thinking. "I expect you're right. All the same, it would be wise to check everyone is in place. Leave by the West entrance at dusk, find the Stranger and get a report. I'll go to Ranu. He can take word to the dogs." The voice was getting fainter, as if its owner were moving away. James strained to catch the words. "The human target is travelling at night, which they doubtless think is safer. We have to strike before they reach their destination so we have all twelve of them together. Make no mistake, Brack, this will be the most significant strike we have made. It *must* go ahead."

"Yes, sir. I'll return to my quarters now."

"Dusk, Brack."

"Dusk, sir."

Evie and Loulou were already heading out of the copse and James, hearing nothing further, ran after them. They were several metres away from the treeline before Loulou spoke.

"You could drop your weapon now, agent."

"What?" Evie looked confused for a second, then remembered the stick she was clutching. "Oh!" She dropped it and started flexing her fingers.

"At least we have the headquarters confirmed." Loulou stated. "The hawk did that for us."

"Hawks speak to badgers then," Evie said.

"Yes," agreed Loulou. "And vice versa. But if you don't have a hawk - or preferably fox – network, which of course we don't …" Loulou didn't need to finish her thought for them.

James had been waiting during this exchange, to deliver his news, and his heart was fluttering around in his chest.

"Agents?" Loulou and Evie turned to face him." I can speak badger, too." James shrugged. "Want to know what they said?"

CHAPTER 25

A LONG DAY BEGINS

WHEN JAMES AND Loulou wandered across to the cottage the following morning, they found a crumpled Michiko slumped across her desk, where she had been all night. Loulou barked once and Michiko sat bolt upright in an instant. She promptly began explaining to Loulou that, having spent most of the night on internet searches, she had at last narrowed down the possibilities. With James' invaluable information – here she positively beamed at James for a moment - she had been able to search for places hosting group meetings in the near future, within a twenty-mile radius of the airport. And she had found it.

"I hacked into the travel manifests for all airlines flying into the airport over the next week. It ended up taking – well, all night, as you saw. So many lists of names. And nationalities. Searching for passengers, researching their professions, their employers … for anything really." Michiko's gaze had started to drift away from them as she spoke. She shook her head. "I *missed it* the first time around. I wasn't expecting it. But then, certain nationalities, just started jumping out at me. So I made a list." She scrabbled about on the desk and held up a piece of A4 which had six names written in bold capital letters, alongside nationalities and professions. Michiko seemed very pleased with herself, though it meant nothing at all to James. He wondered suddenly if Loulou could even read. Michiko was still speaking.

"So then I went searching for the other three, of course, and there they were – all arriving within a couple of hours of each other. All scheduled to leave together by coach."

Michiko turned the piece of paper around and James saw nine countries, each with a neat tick beside it: America, China, Russia, France, India, Israel, Pakistan, North Korea, the UK.

"The other three people were easy. I found an interpreter, a British government official and a personal assistant. So there you have it! Twelve people in all. Well, and a driver I suppose." Michiko had stood up to display her findings but now lowered herself slowly back into the chair. Loulou walked around the desk and nudged Michiko's hand, speaking to her.

"You, agent, should be very proud. We just need to know a little bit more, then I suggest you sleep, properly. Can you tell us where and when they will sabotage them?"

"Oh." Michiko said. James thought he had never seen anyone look quite as tired. "Well, no … The coach is scheduled for the conference centre at Ingleside. For a seminar on 'Economics' apparently. But obviously they're all countries that hold nuclear weapons, so –"

"Yes, quite." Loulou said. James realised he was a bystander again, with no part to play in this conversation. It all sounded very serious. Michiko was still talking and he tried to concentrate. He wanted to remember everything so he could ask questions later.

"No mention in the media of a nuclear summit. Whatever it is, it's secret. I called Singh already, but – no, we don't know when and where Loulou – that's the thing we don't know. That's what we need to know." Loulou's voice suddenly became very school teacher-ish as she replied.

"Right. You have done amazingly. But now - bed, two hours at least. James?"

"Yes?" he said, startled to be addressed at all.

"If lessons have finished, you need to come outside. It's time for P.E."

Inside his wooden shack, the Stranger sat at a laptop while a small electric generator hummed away in the corner. Just inside the door, a badger shuffled from side to side, never coming further into the room.

"It doesn't bite, Brack," the man snapped. The badger stepped forward the tiniest amount. "You can tell Titan that all three flights are on schedule and due to land between ten and midnight. In other words, the coach will leave the airport on time. Actually, just tell him that. 'The coach is on time.'" He glanced down at the badger as he said this last part, speaking each word slowly and clearly.

The badger shuffled backwards to leave. The Stranger grabbed a shabby old backpack and followed the badger out, pausing to check the door to the shack had locked securely as he did so. The badger was several feet away when the man called after him.

"I'll send another message, before dawn."

Ranu was a fox who hated humans, as most did. For generations foxes had had their brushes hacked off as trophies while vixens and cubs were left deserted. Then when the vixens went to hunt, they ran the risk of being killed too, and leaving motherless cubs. Humans fenced off swathes of territory and effectively removed the foxes' natural prey, so Ranu's kind had begun to venture onto farms and steal chickens. If they were caught, they were shot.

The situation had become so dire that many foxes were abandoning their homes and skulking around the outskirts of towns, snatching food from dustbins. It was degrading, and Ranu despised the creatures many foxes had become – all through man's interference: claiming the land, building, fencing, then killing. Foxes had been a respected species in the past and Ranu, for one, longed for the past to return.

All he could do, however, was try to hurt mankind as they had hurt him and being a Misant was the only way to do that. So here he was, delivering a message from a badger to a dog. Ranu disliked dogs intensely, which was unsurprising given their history, but he could speak to them. He trusted in the hope that their common cause was stronger than any instinct.

Ranu slowed his running as the hedgerow he was following met the wood-and-mesh fence of a garden. He stopped and yipped loudly. Immediately a dog started barking and a human voice yelled.

"Get 'im, boy, go on!"

Ranu stood his ground with his heart bouncing against his chest, leg muscles tensed.

A squat, muscular shape thundered down the length of the garden and thudded to a halt with the metre high fence between them. The bulldog barked and growled, identifying himself, then – as Ranu told him the message – he repeated it, loudly.

"Operation going ahead tonight. All operatives meet at bridge for orders." The bulldog grunted his approval. "Go safely, comrade."

Ranu left as quietly as he had arrived, while the bulldog went lumbering back up the garden path to the sound of:

"Good lad, that's the way!"

After allowing the old man to pat him vigorously on the head, the bulldog wandered out to the front of the house. A large crow swooped down to within a few feet and snapped:

"I have the message already. I should think every speaker in the neighbourhood does! I'll head off now. You should send it groundwards too, though, just in case." The bulldog snorted in agreement and remained where he was watching the crow become a dot in the grey sky. A moment later, a mottled black-and-white tom cat stuck its head through the bottom of the privet hedge. The bulldog huffed, a half-bark.

"News?" The cat asked, shortly. The bulldog repeated his message and told the cat to spread the word to as many Misant operatives as possible.

"Going now." The Tom spat, and left.

The bulldog sighed noisily, his work done, and plodded back to the rear of the house where he snacked on some dog biscuits and water. His owner, who had been struggling and failing to start an electric lawnmower all this time, shoved the machine aside and cursed.

"New-fangled things," he said. "Better off without them."

He grabbed a scythe that had been leaning against the shed wall and trudged purposefully off down the garden. His bulldog, settling down for a nap in the quiet, muttered:

"I couldn't agree more."

James was sitting at the kitchen table, with headphones in, trying to concentrate on World War Two history and making typos as he responded to his tutor. Loulou, Gizmo, Evie and Rags were playing frisbee in the field. Loulou had said it was a great way to improve reflexes for Evie. James' mind was flying around the field with the frisbee too. He suddenly realised the tutor was setting homework so he cut-and-pasted the conversation into his History folder, clicked on his classmates to say goodbye, and hit shutdown.

"Everything OK, Mitch?" Ash's head had popped around the kitchen door. Michiko was in there too, pouring herself a strong, black coffee. She considered Ash for a moment, then blinked and seemed to find the contents of her coffee mug more interesting.

"Sure." She sighed. "I just need to borrow Agent Loulou for a minute. I need another perspective. Could you fetch her for me, do you think?"

"No probs," said Ash, and went outside. James watched through the window as Loulou heard Ash calling her and loped swiftly across the grass to the cottage.

"Ah, agent," Michiko greeted her. James had by now realised that Agent Michiko always started the day beautifully groomed, with her hair and clothes perfectly neat and tidy. It was, therefore, possible to judge – just from her appearance – how the day was going. Right now, Michiko's blouse had come untucked on one side, and she was twisting a strand of hair round and round her fingers as she worked but, other than that, she seemed OK.

"Right." Michiko leaned against the table, cradling her coffee. "The delegates' coach will arrive at one o'clock in the morning at the centre. I think whatever is planned will happen during the journey itself … We know when they are travelling, what vehicle they will be in, and where they are heading. There only seems to be one likely route. They could make a detour but I can't think why they would. They appear to have deliberately chosen a road with very little, if any, traffic at that hour of the night. So, there's just one variable now."

"Where," said Loulou.

"Exactly." Michiko's forehead furrowed. "I hope you won't take it amiss, agent, but I thought you might have a closer perspective. If there are no human Misants involved, I am wondering how – and please forgive me – but, how a group of animals could manage to stop a large moving vehicle, much less cause it any danger."

James considered this. He imagined a pack of dogs running out into the road, or maybe larger animals? Cows, or sheep? But that might be a suicide mission and even then a coach might not stop… He listened again.

"…so that leads me to believe there must be humans involved, so I've been looking at using another vehicle perhaps. But then I think, what if that's the only angle I consider and it turns out to be the wrong one? So I need to think of every possibility. So, then I come back to creature-based activity –" Michiko ran her hand over her head from front to back, so her fringe lifted up slightly. James watched Loulou following the movement of Michiko's hand. She interrupted.

"And you are going round in circles, because it's so important you get it right." Michiko nodded. "I appreciate your asking for my opinion agent. We know there are very few human Misants. But we do know of this man they call 'Stranger' and, if they have even one human onboard, they would be fools not to use him. So I believe we are guaranteed one man at least." Michiko nodded, studying Loulou, who continued talking in a low, thoughtful growl. "Personally, I think another vehicle would be the most logical idea. It might be possible to run the coach off the road, though perhaps not to guarantee significant injury to all passengers. But –" Loulou stopped and sniffed at James' tablet, still on the kitchen table. "But my gut tells me that's not the way Misants think. They are hardly likely to use mankind's technology by *choice*, even to further their cause. As a last resort, but not as an *initial* plan."

"So …?" Michiko let the word hang.

"So indeed." Loulou said. "So … you need to be searching for somewhere they could create an ambush. They will need to surprise the driver, damage the coach – the tyres maybe. But it would have to be somewhere where that would matter – just running it off the road might not be sufficient to do enough damage …"

James imagined the coach running suddenly off the road – and plunging –

"A river!" he said, jumping up. "Is there a river?"

Michiko had been on her phone zooming in on a map, while Loulou was talking, clicking on photos of areas along the route.

"Oh – *yes, there is*," she hissed through gritted teeth, looking up, from James to Loulou and back. "And – a bridge."

"Ah," said Loulou thoughtfully. "A bridge. I think we have it then."

She padded over to James and, to his enormous surprise, gave the back of his hand a big, wet lick.

CHAPTER 26

A LONG NIGHT BEGINS

THIS WAS IT. Everyone in the van was quiet. James realised he was glad Evie was there – someone else who was a newcomer and had never done anything like this before. James had the distinct feeling that if Mum knew he was heading out in the post office van with the team, to intercept a Misant group – well, he wouldn't be. No-one had mentioned telling her and James decided not to bring it up. He had texted as usual, told her he had done classes today and played frisbee. James knew he would have to tell her about the rest of it when he returned but, by then, it would be too late to say 'no'. He swallowed down the hollow feeling he discovered in his stomach, despite having eaten a short while ago.

"We'll stop half a mile North of the bridge, Rags. There's a turning on the map, a track I suppose – it's not much – but it'll be enough to pull the van off the road. Then we'll separate – teams of two or three." This was Michiko, back in charge. James found her soldierly voice oddly comforting. "We need to be there early to make sure this is the place. If it isn't, we'll just have to back-track in the van and hope we catch the coach before they do. Then I guess our best bet is to drive along with it, but that's going to be hard to explain. Let's hope this is the spot." Michiko sighed, wrinkling her forehead and plucking at her jacket pocket, which turned inside out.

"What are we looking for when we get there?" Evie asked.

"Misants!" Agent Michiko replied. James felt his mouth start to smirk and covered it with his hand, coughing a little. "Or anything odd. There may be some sort of booby-trap rigged up. Whatever it is, we have to find it. But, whatever it is, it will probably be guarded. I'm afraid we'll be thinking on our feet." Evie nodded. Their expressions were all very serious, even Ash's - who was crammed in the back seat with James and Evie. "When anyone does find anything, call me immediately. I'll bring everyone to you." Michiko instructed them.

James and the others all lapsed back into thought, until the van bumped off the road and ground to a halt in a small, stony lay-by, lined by trees. Rags pulled the van in close, under the branches. He had had the headlights on but, when he switched them off, James noticed it was rapidly becoming pretty dark: the humans had all packed torches. Michiko decided that Loulou, Gizmo and James would stay together, Ash would accompany Evie, and Rags with Michiko. If they were to come across Misant operatives, two dogs were a better bet than two humans, so Loulou was to take the lead in searching around the bridge itself. If they had to, they would explain James' presence somehow – but Loulou had decided it would be more useful to have him with them than not, because of his creaturespeak ability. James suspected it also had something to do with her promise to Mum.

The remaining humans were paired to try to even up their experience. Michiko had informed them that, strictly speaking, neither Rags nor Gizmo ought to be leaving the van. But both Gizmo and Loulou being around would help as cover if they were surprised by any Misants, and Rags was certainly not about to be left behind.

The road was quiet once they had parked. James imagined, when it was fully dark, it would be pretty hard to see at all. The bridge spanned the river

Coln, and they could hear its water chattering in the background. The river swept away from them, cold and dark, and James shuddered.

"You OK James?" Agent Ash asked.

"Sure," James replied, forcing cheerfulness into his voice. "Just a bit chilly for a moment." Ash winked, then gave him a 'thumbs up'.

"Evie, Ash," Michiko said. "I want you to travel back up the road away from the bridge. I need forewarning of anything coming towards us from the South. If the coach is earlier than anticipated, or we haven't found the trap, I want to know when it's coming."

"OK, agent," Evie confirmed. "And if we spot anything unusual we'll call you." The two set off up the darkening road.

"Rags and I will head higher up." Michiko said. "We'll be able to see a little for another half hour or so. Higher ground is usually advantageous, so it's likely they'll have a base of some sort up there. The idea is for us to *not* be seen, this is recon only at the moment. Agent Loulou, if you could head down the bank near the river and walk half a mile in each direction, Rags and I will come down on the other bank and do the same. James, can you swim?" James' eyes popped wide as he answered.

"Ye-es …"

"Just as well. But stay clear of the river anyway, please. It's night and it has a current. Do not go near enough to endanger yourself. It would endanger the mission too, remember. Just stay close to Agent Loulou. Clear?" James nodded his head rapidly. It was very clear indeed.

The group split up and James headed down towards the shadowy riverbank, a dog on either side. He touched Loulou's back with his fingers for reassurance and she walked a fraction closer to him so he could feel her big, warm presence.

"I'll just follow your lead, agent," Gizmo sounded totally calm. As they reached the bank, the little terrier fell in step just behind them; Loulou was on the river side, James next to the grass and open country. The world felt very empty. Once they were on a level with the river, the roadway was high above them and James could not begin to spot where the others might be. He pulled his phone out of his pocket and, careful to shield the light from the screen, flicked it on to check the time. It was nearly nine o'clock. It was then he noticed the signal bar. It was blank.

"Loulou!" James whispered.

"Yes?" She answered quietly.

"My phone's not working – there's no signal!" James felt his stomach flutter as he realised it was very likely there was no signal where the rest of the group was either. Loulou did not slow her stride.

It's a good thing we have you then, isn't it? James realised Loulou was not speaking out loud.

Oh! He replied in the same way. *But I can just speak to you, anyway – what do we do about the others?*

Loulou's voice in his head felt somehow warm and friendly, as she said: *You can speak to them too, can't you? If you heard the badgers underground, there's no reason you can't speak to, say, Evie in the open air – even if she is half a mile away.* James was unsure. He had never attempted this. *Try it,* Loulou suggested. James took a deep breath in, through his nose, and breathed out very slowly between his lips. He pictured Evie and faced the direction of the road. He concentrated hard, imagining himself yelling out Evie's name as loudly as he could. Nothing happened, but he focussed even harder, and tried again.

Evie and Ash were walking along opposite sides of the road, peering into the darkness around them and listening, though Evie for one was unsure of what they were looking and listening for. Evie was furthest ahead when she suddenly jumped and whipped her head round, yelling out, as someone screamed her name.

"What the –!" She continued to swing around, turning a quick full circle. "Where are you?"

Ash ran a few steps. "Hey – I'm right here." He said. "What's the matter?"

"Not you - *him!*" Ash's face fell blank. Evie stared at him. "*James!* Where is he?" Ash placed his hand lightly on her arm, saying:

"He went down to the river, remember, with Agent Loulou?"

Evie snatched her arm away. She was peering far out into the darkness hoping to spot the boy she had just heard. Out of the corner of her eye she noticed Ash reach for his mobile.

"Oh, *what!* Not *again!*" Evie heard James' voice calling her, even louder. "What? *What?* Oh. Oh no. Ash – have you checked your phone?" she said. "There's no signal, is there?"

"No."

"It's alright," Evie said.

"Is it?" Said Ash.

"I can contact James without the phone. He's speaking to me now. If I focus on him he'll hear me. Then he can talk to Agent Michiko. So we don't need the phone. Apparently." Evie stopped talking and felt her shoulders drop as all the air seemed to drain out of her. Evie watched Ash's face gradually break into a grin.

"Ooh!" He said. "It was *James!* You heard him! In your head."

"Yes," Evie said. "And I'm *so* not cool with it. He's gone, for now. Let's get on with this. I reckon we can turn around in a few minutes ... Come on!" Evie resumed her purposeful march up the dark road. After a moment she heard Ash's footsteps patting the road surface as he jogged to catch up, but she ignored him when he said:

"Well *I* think it's pretty darn cool."

As James, Loulou and Gizmo padded along the riverbank, James became aware of muttering voices somewhere in the darkness. He silently conveyed this news to both Loulou and Gizmo. The little terrier seemed entirely unsurprised to hear James talking inside his head.

Thanks for the warning. Keep in touch. Gizmo's voice smiled as he strolled along. Loulou had clearly been thinking and responded:

James, your sub-verbal hearing is better than ours - but some of them may be hearing us by now too. If we leave, I think it will be more suspicious than if we stay. I think we need to pretend we're here with them. We need to pretend we're Misants. Loulou had been sniffing for different scents as they walked. *It seems to me they are dotted about, keeping to their own kinds.* James had been concentrating on snatches of conversation here and there.

Yes – I can hear a couple of voices, then there's a gap, then there are more. I can hear someone now up ahead.

Good, Loulou said. *Right, we need to do the same as them. Find a spot and wait. Move out into the grass, James.* He did so, at the same time telling Gizmo that they were now undercover Misants. The three settled down to see what would happen next. James could sense animals in the darkness all around him. He suddenly thought about sitting in the park for summer evening concerts with Mum: the same sort of quiet groups, chatting, waiting. Except here it was darker, and a bit cold, and he was with Loulou. After a moment they heard a voice.

"Hello? Dogs and human, can you hear me?"

"Of course," answered Loulou. "Who are you?"

"Are you here for the bridge?"

"Why else?" Loulou said. The voice moved closer. James, surprised, had already recognised the scent and sound of a fox. He knew Gizmo had too, by the tension throughout his small body.

"The human with you – is it the Stranger?" The voice sounded eager.

"What? Oh – no," Loulou said. "He's just a Misant child. His parents are, are nearby, but the boy speaks well and we thought he might be useful - in these, er, circumstances. We haven't met the Stranger – is he supposed to be here?" The fox's voice was fainter now. He appeared to be moving away, having checked out their little group.

"Yes. He'll come. Wait." The fox had returned to his group and Gizmo visibly relaxed. Loulou spoke to James in low voice so Gizmo would hear.

"James, I need you to tell Agents Michiko and Evie what just happened and what we are doing. Then tell me what our orders are. Can you do that?" James said he thought so and began to picture Agent Michiko with her spiky hair and worried expression. He had no difficulty at all in reaching her. He explained their current position. Michiko's response rang out, loud and shrill inside his skull.

"*How many* Misants?"

CHAPTER 27

A SIMPLE PLAN

THE STRANGER HAD a very simple plan. He intended for the coach carrying the representatives to crash. He intended that crash to take place on a bridge with a significant drop. And if that wasn't sufficient to do the job, then the river water below ought to ensure that no-one escaped. He expected the representatives to die in the crash or, at the very least, to be badly injured. He didn't much care which. The crash would of course make news headlines and the resulting chaos could only work in the Misants' favour.

He had not yet decided which Eco group he would choose to name as responsible, but he knew the reason "they" would give was that destructive technologies could not be allowed to continue. The nine representatives were not political officials, they were actual scientists: the higher-ups who personally engineered these weapons, meeting in secret, away from the eyes of the world. This made them the perfect target, all in one place: he would destroy those who created the technology of destruction. It would serve as a warning to others who might think to take their places.

No-one would ever know where the ambush had come from. There would be no human trail to trace. It was a beautiful way to spread fear among humans. The Stranger could only thank fate for having provided him with such a rare chance. He found it curious that non-creaturespeaking humans went to so much trouble to retain their secrets, when the biggest secret was kept firmly from them all. Misants were as good as invisible to most humans and the Stranger fully intended to use that invisibility to change the way the world operated, one mission at a time. This coach was just the first step.

Now, the Stranger was walking along a dark road approaching the bridge from the South, with a fox at his heels and a barn owl softly brushing the air above him, circling to keep pace.

"Report, Cladrin," the Stranger ordered. The owl swept down, ghost-like.

"Groups of land creatures along the river, the bridge central to them all. Nothing flying except bats. We have fox, badger, dog, cat, weasel and stoat." The

Stranger had to admit to himself that old Titan had been correct after all. Loyalty to the cause had indeed brought them out in packs.

After Evie received a message from James about the Misants grouped by the river, Agent Ash started to scan the skies. Evie was about to ask what he was looking for when she suddenly dropped to a crouch, ducking. A whistle of air had swept over her head, close enough to be felt. Agent Sheera landed infront of Ash, and Evie slowly stood up, breathing out.

"Not just luck, I take it?" She asked Ash.

"Nah. Good idea though, wasn't it? Mitch is going to thank me for this one," He chuckled. "Sheera – you are an angel in raven form, girl. We need a hand."

"You do," Agent Sheera said. "There's a baahrn owl circling a huuman about a mile from herrre, and it wohn't be long beforrre she rounds that hiiill on one of her forrrward sorties. She'll see yoou as clear as dahhy, especially since you're moooving. You need to get under coverrr quiiick."

Ash glanced at Evie. They had turned round several minutes ago and were now heading back towards the bridge.

"Van!" They said in unison and started to jog.

"Sheera," Ash called softly. "Michiko and Rags are up top – can you get them to the van too?" The raven did not trouble to respond but took off and was invisible in a second.

A very few minutes later they were back in the van, with Michiko, who spoke in hushed tones.

"I should have checked in with Singh two hours ago, so someone somewhere will be searching for us by now... *Why* didn't I make sure there was network coverage?" Evie thought Michiko looked ill.

"Yeah, but you've got to love the irony," Ash said. "Being let down by technology, and facing a group of Misants?"

Evie glared at Ash thinking he could really do with a lesson on when to shut up.

James had been staring up at the stars, thinking of all the space between him and them, when he had felt the owl speaking to someone. He had told Loulou and she instructed him to get under the bridge quickly. She and Gizmo had followed at a more leisurely pace, discussing out loud how even Misant humans still liked their shelter. They joined James where he was sitting, cross-legged in precisely the middle of the bridge width.

"Can you still hear it?" Loulou said. James listened. A shiver ran down his body and he felt cold inside.

"What is it James?"

"I just heard a man. He asked the owl for a report." James listened again and felt himself relax slightly. "It didn't see me. I must have been under the bridge before he flew over. But the man – it's him isn't it? It's the Stranger." Before Loulou could respond, Michiko's voice brushed the edge of his consciousness and he allowed it in.

James? We have returned to the van to be out of sight. If we cannot sabotage this event, Rags intends to drive towards the coach and, when we meet it, Rags will steer towards it deliberately. The coach should stop, which will allow Rags to ram it pretty accurately. The intention is to do only enough damage to disable their vehicle's headlights. Rags will then claim to have fallen asleep at the wheel. The rest of us will remain hidden.

She paused and James imagined her raking her hands through her hair yet again. *It's hardly ideal as we will then have to drive away from the scene in order find a phone signal. We just hope it will be sufficient to make the Misants change their minds.*

Stay hidden and safe until I call you. James relayed this whole message to the other two.

"Agent Loulou – the Stranger ..." He wasn't sure what he wanted to say. After coming so far, to drive away without even seeing the man was too terrible to contemplate. If the Stranger truly was a stranger, then James would be putting himself and his friends at risk by revealing his presence.

But if the Stranger was his Dad – what then? Surely his own father could never do him any harm? And yet surely his own father could never be a leader of Misants intending terrible harm to a coachload of humans. James was still trying to find some words to explain any of this when Loulou spoke first.

"I know James, but you have to stay hidden if possible. You are here to listen. If there is a chance to see him, I will help you to do that I promise, but first we need to understand his plan in case we can still do something to stop it – however many Misants there are." *Except I have never been quite so entirely surrounded and outnumbered by Misants, much less with a child at my side.*

James was about to reply when he realised Loulou had merely been thinking to herself and had no idea at all that she had communicated her fears to James.

Mr T and Zed had been tracking James' team ever since they left Ops South, watching the little dots move here and there, many miles away. Three days in, however, the EagleView signal had started to glitch. Zed explained to Mr T that this was not unusual. He was bouncing a signal off a satellite some 24,000 miles away up in space – there were plenty of possibilities for interference. It could be trees, hills, clouds, anything. Given the importance of the people they were following, however, Mr T felt uneasy every time the dots winked out – even though the signal always returned minutes later. When Zed received a call from Agent Singh suggesting that he might like to join his grandson as soon as possible, though, Mr T became properly concerned. Zed put the call on speaker.

"What have you heard, Agent Singh?"

"More than rumours at last." Agent Singh said. "Agent Michiko confirmed the target group earlier today and is currently heading to the most likely area for an ambush. The coach concerned is not due to arrive there for another couple of hours, but here's the thing: I've lost comms." Singh coughed then continued. "I, er, tried to phone Michiko but I'm not getting through. I needed to tell her a call has gone out for all Misant operatives in the area to meet at the bridge - *all operatives*, Zed, Mr T? This Stranger is then going to lead them in some sort of … sabotage act." Singh's voice cracked a little now as he spoke and, from the slight echo, Mr T could imagine him pacing up and down. "I expected maybe a handful of Misants … I can't think what this plan of theirs is about. They surely don't intend to *reveal* co-operation between creatures? I can't imagine the public chaos if they do! I have notified Ops Wales, but agents Teegan and Rhys are down in St Davids dealing with something, so it'll take them at least three hours to get back - it's just too long."

"I can do it in half that," Zed cut in. "I'll call you from Ops West. I'll have Em and T with me." Mr T had blinked his agreement from where he sat on the desk, ears twitching with the vibrations of the speakerphone.

"I want you to get Agent Artemis too. She wants in. I think she's still pretty mad about their last encounter." Agent Singh paused before adding: "He's in *good* company you know - Loulou is no fool and Agent Michiko runs a pretty tight ship."

"Yes I know, Singh, but what are we up against? I need to see this so-called *Stranger.*" Part way through the call, Mr T had noticed Em standing by the door to Ops, clutching Zed's leather jacket and helmet. Agent Zed swung around as she said:

"I called Helen. I told her they had located the target zone and that we were going up to look after James overnight. She'll come in here tomorrow as usual to keep an eye on Ops."

Mr T and Zed exchanged a glance, while Em pursed her lips, each knowing that what Em had told Helen was only a shadow of the truth. But now was definitely not the time for discussion – so they had hit the road, the bike's GPS giving Zed plenty of warning about speed traps, and Mr T bracing himself inside the carrier as the bike accelerated.

By the time they collected Agent Artemis Mr T was feeling travelsick, though he was determined not to actually *be* sick, especially as he was now sharing the somewhat confined quarters of the box on the back of the Harley. They had been travelling for some time and yet Artemis seemed utterly at home in their mode of transport, alternately sleeping and chatting along the way. Mr T mainly concentrated on not seeing out of the window. He was delighted when at last he felt the bike juddering to a halt on a scree of small stones, as Agent Zed pulled up outside Ops West. Agent Em climbed down from the pillion and stretched her arms out wide before leaning backwards with her hands on her hips.

"So," Em said, removing her helmet and hanging it over a handle bar. "It's another half an hour from here?"

"Yep." Zed had released Mr T and Artemis from the passenger box, and they had jumped down, Mr T being slightly unsteady as he hit the ground.

"We'll have a scout round," Artemis said. "If you can check inside, Zed?"

"Sure," Agent Zed replied. "Hope I can get in without breaking a window." Mr T caught Em smiling as she walked over to the front door and tried it. When it didn't open, she lifted the flower pot beside the step, removed a key from underneath it, and unlocked the front door.

"Zed, dear, welcome to the countryside." She grinned, leading the way in. Mr T and Artemis headed round to the back of the house but after a few minutes they slipped in through a window Em had flung open, in time to see Zed replace a phone on the desk.

"You need to come outside," Mr T said. "There's an agent with a message."

In the garden there was a large raven, revealed by an outside light, perched on the drystone wall. She introduced herself as Agent Sheera, and delivered her message, before swooping wearily up towards the trees. Within ten minutes of their arrival, the four agents were all back on the bike and roaring along the country lanes again. Mr T closed his eyes until they were just slits, pretending to sleep, and concentrated on anything except the scenery that was whizzing past.

CHAPTER 28

BATTLEGROUND

TWELVE PASSENGERS FOR Ingleside boarded the coach, which was in fact just a fourteen-seater minibus with very plush seats. The passengers were tired from their flights and, some of them, from the time change. Each was quietly anticipating reaching his or her hotel room. The passengers could all speak English, but conversation was scarce and the warmth of the coach coupled with the comforting hum of the engine soon had people's heads nodding into cushioned seatbacks. The driver checked his group in the mirror, clicked "Start" on the satnav, and carefully pulled away from the kerb.

James was listening to words ringing out into the darkness from the Stranger, completing a speech to all those spread along the riverbank.

"… and groups like ours will then take action all across the Earth, because they will see what can be done by putting aside our differences and acting as one." The Stranger paused, scanning the darkness. The night was silent and, to James, the air felt as if it were charged with electricity. "You must now move up to the road – Ranu here will lead you. Act quickly, as soon as all its wheels are *on* the bridge – all of you, at the same time, together! *For the Cause!*"

"For the Cause!" Voices from along the bank echoed the Stranger's words in yips and cries. The darkness began to ripple as a number of shadowy forms made their way to the appointed spot, following the fox.

James had been relaying all of this to Michiko, who told him Loulou was to follow the Misant group, but break away and slip back towards the van. James and Gizmo were to remain where they were when the group left, but Rags would join them.

Evie listened to Michiko explaining that she wanted the civilians safely together, hidden and out of harm's way. Her latest plan was to disrupt the Misants before the coach ever reached the bridge.

James had estimated the Misant force at well over fifty animals, ranging from Doberman to stoat. Michiko had a Post Office van, three humans and a Bernese Mountain dog. Evie placed both hands on the back of Loulou's seat and gripped it. Loulou spoke, calmly.

"Agent Michiko, we are all with you." Evie nodded, and Ash added:

"We sure are, boss – go for it."

Evie, seated in the back, watched Michiko's face – reflected in the rear-view mirror, her mouth a thin line. Michiko grasped the steering wheel and – keeping the headlights off – turned on the ignition.

James watched Rags scrabble down to join him and Gizmo, then heard the engine of the van start to hum faintly, becoming a louder rumble as the vehicle approached. The people surrounding Ranu were exchanging glances. They heard the engine immediately, but it was not what they had expected. It was from the wrong direction for a start. They began questioning amongst themselves.

"Is this it?"

"What should we do?"

"We should move!"

"It can't be, though, it's the wrong way."

"But what if it is?"

Evie trusted in Michiko to use all her senses to keep the van on the road, as the engine became a roar, accelerating towards the bridge in darkness. Without slowing down, Michiko flipped on the headlights' full beam, revealing a pack of creatures grouped as one at the North end of the bridge on the grass beside the road. She swung the steering wheel hard over heading directly into the group. At the same time, she jammed her foot on the brake for all she was worth, muttering to herself:

"Move, move, move, move …"

Caught by the whiteness of the glare, animals flew in confusion in all directions, scattered like shockwaves, seeming terrified by the explosion of light and noise. Evie, like Ash, was still clinging tightly to the seatbacks, Loulou had wedged herself on the floor in the front, but Michiko was fully focused on wrestling the steering wheel to gain control of the rattling, crashing, sliding vehicle as it shuddered to a stop - and stalled. The van rocked, and hung at an angle for a long moment during which Evie shared a wide-eyed stare with Ash, before it collapsed slowly sideways, then thumped loudly to the ground, echoing like a gigantic drum.

When all movement ceased, Evie saw Michiko push her palms upwards to heave open the driver's door that was now at an angle above her. Pulling herself up and out with some effort, she slid down outside. Evie heard her land with a wet thud on the muddy ground, churned by the sliding tyres. The van's rear doors had split apart so Evie and Ash crawled out through them, followed by the solid bulk of Loulou, who appeared completely unhurt. Evie could feel bruises in all sorts of places, and even Ash was silent, bent double trying to catch his breath. The van's headlights were still illuminating a large swathe of river and field.

In the shadows, and on the edges of the light, was chaos. The smaller, more timid animals had clearly fled, melting away into the darkness. Evie caught sight of some of them scurrying, until they vanished. She felt a small surge of triumph rise within her. The larger animals, however, were gradually returning to the scene, she realised. The general hum of confusion was now being overpowered by a

Doberman who was barking instructions to anyone who would listen:

"They are *Lifelink operatives!* Attack!"

An extremely large badger lumbered closer to the van and called:

"Keep to the plan, cowards! *Hold fast!*"

Then a fox appeared from the darkness and took up the call.

"Fight comrades, fight for the cause!"

Evie and the other Lifelink agents moved together, the fallen van behind them, surveying the angry crowd that was approaching. Something Agent Zed had said niggled at the back of Evie's mind. She felt trapped against the van. Almost automatically, she began to run.

"Here!" yelled Evie. "This way!"

She turned and backed up the bank, seeing the others following her. They were now slightly above their attackers but still within the band of brightness from the van's lights. Evie figured that most of their attackers could see them just as well in the dark, so they had nothing to lose and everything to gain by illuminating the battleground. Because - it dawned on her with a sickening lurch of her stomach -

battleground was exactly what it was. Evie was grasping a wooden mallet in her hand, which she had seen in the rear of the van amongst Rags' tools. It was as if her hands had simply known she would need a weapon, as she had no recollection of picking it up. Ash, Evie saw, was clutching a tyre iron.

Evie glanced around then darted to the very edge of the circle of light where there was something in the grass. She was rewarded by finding a branch, broken and discarded. She weighed it in one hand, the mallet in the other, then snapped the end off the branch to leave it jagged. Rushing over to Michiko, who had now picked herself up and joined the others, Evie thrust the makeshift weapon into her grateful hands. The four agents made a semi-circle facing the angry mob, which had banded back together and was nearly upon them.

There was no time to think as the Doberman shot forward, breaking the tension like an explosion, and heading straight for the most dangerous looking Lifelink operative. Loulou, however, hit him head on – like a wall of fur – and the two dogs became a writhing ball of growling fury.

Evie and Ash exchanged a desperate look and took a joint step forward to meet the remaining group. It seemed only the bravest of the Misants had remained to join the fight. They were an odd bunch: the Doberman, a fox, the badger, a couple of feral cats, two largish mongrels and, apparently, a couple of bats that flew at the humans' heads any time they twisted into the darkness. The rest of the Misants hung back in the shadows, watching.

Evie saw Ash stride forward to meet their attackers and the snarling mongrels leapt at him. He raised the iron bar and caught one dog a blow on the shoulder that knocked him off course, making him skid backwards a few feet before bunching himself up and springing forward again. His partner, head down, was going for Ash's ankles and trying to knock him to the floor.

Evie had been distracted for a second by the sudden fights whirling around her, but was brought rudely back her senses. She felt pain shoot through her shin, screamed, and beat her mallet down towards the head of a fox. At the same time, she kicked at him in retaliation for the nasty bite he had just inflicted. Already shaking with nerves at what was happening around her, Evie now felt hot adrenalin burning through her arms and legs as she backed further uphill and began hitting out at the various animal forms gathering around her.

The smaller of the mongrels changed target and went for Agent Michiko who was now standing, back-to-back with Evie, trying to fend off the group of creatures who took turns darting in at them – apparently testing their defences, trying to throw them off balance. Evie was truly petrified. She clung desperately to the lessons Zed and Loulou had provided and held her ground. The mongrel disappeared again and Evie heard Ash curse out loud, his voice a snarl of fury. Turning, Michiko stumbled on the uneven ground and as she fell the badger began barrelling towards her. Evie yelled and struggled to bat her way past the animals surrounding her and blocking her path. The two cats took turns to run in and slash at Evie's legs. One of them leapt at her, digging its claws in, getting a vicious hold through the denim of her jeans before she threw it off. The Misants were obviously intending for Evie to fall, too.

Just before the badger could fasten its jaws on Michiko's terrified face, a small, brown and white missile shot up the bank and hit the badger firmly in the flank, sinking its teeth into the side of the much larger animal. The badger roared and turned aside from Michiko, who scrambled, panic-stricken, to her feet – just in time to engage the smaller mongrel once again.

The badger writhed and flung itself onto its side managing to dislodge Gizmo, who was knocked back, but leapt at the badger again immediately. The badger hit him with his massive paw and four red welts scored across Gimo's belly, bright in the van lights. Evie felt hot tears welling up inside her, as she swung angrily at the snarling fox, which yelped and backed off.

Everywhere, the night was filled with awful sounds: yelping, snarling, panting for breath and screaming in pain. It was almost impossible to tell what shriek was human and what animal, until a massive, unearthly howl turned everyone's head.

Evie saw Loulou collapse, limp, with the Doberman standing over her, his body shaking, his flanks bloody and heaving. There was a split second's pause, during which the three humans found themselves grouped together again, with the churning river behind them. Evie's heart was pounding on her rib cage, trying to escape, and the darkness of the night seemed to press in further on the fading circle of light. Evie knew she was muttering the word "no", over and over, but could not stop.

The mongrels and Doberman were re-grouping, joining one another, growling low and continuously, advancing step by step towards the agents. Behind them were the fox and the feral cats. Gizmo and the badger were still locked in combat, with the little dog returning again and again to be beaten by the ferocious larger animal. The remaining group ignored them, however, preparing for a battle of their own. The Doberman's growl suddenly became a bark and he launched himself towards Ash, who was in the centre of the three. Ash raised the bar in his hand.

As he did, the barking was eclipsed by a much louder roaring noise as a blinding new light split the darkness. A black Harley Davidson swept over the bridge and onto the grass, skidding to a stop and clipping the unsuspecting badger as it did so. Two leather-clad humans dismounted, flinging their helmets aside, while one flipped open the carrier on the back of the bike before running towards the bloodied group.

A grey shape slipped out of the box and landed almost on top of the recoiling badger. Gizmo was lying nearby on the grass, blood seeping from the various rents in his side opened up by the badger's massive claws. The badger, seeing his chance, opened his mouth to savage Gizmo one last time with his massively muscled jaw, but Agent Artemis leaped, landing smoothly and silently between the badger and the prone dog.

The badger made a sound that Evie could only describe as a sneer and raised a paw to sweep the cat away. Artemis raised her paw, too, calmly swiping her prosthetic claws easily through the thick flesh of the badger's nose with an almightily strong blow.

The badger shrieked, in agony and shock, wobbled, and struggled to find his feet before stumbling away, streaming blood, mewling into the night.

The Doberman, who had flipped in mid-spring when the Harley arrived, turned to face the new threat. Evie saw Agent Zed, who had a torch in one hand and what looked like a baseball bat in the other, march directly at the lead dog, yelling and shining the torch into the dog's eyes while raising his weapon.

Agent Em hurried up behind him. In her hands were two rocks apparently gathered up from the roadside. She threw them, one after another, the first one hitting its mark squarely as it caught the larger mongrel on the side of the head, the second skimming the fox's shoulders and causing him to run backwards, stumbling, until he fell over, turned and ran. The feral cats slunk silently into the shadows.

The remaining three dogs began to back away, snarling. The Misant audience had already disappeared from the shadows as if, Evie thought to herself, Zed had raised a magic wand rather than a baseball bat.

"Get away now, and live!" Zed roared. "Or stay –" and he raised the baseball bat higher over the dogs' heads as they cowed down on the grass, retreating. Reaching the edges of the light, they turned, running into the darkness. Only the bats were left, flapping angrily overhead.

The humans turned towards each other. Evie saw faces full of exhaustion and despair, before limping over to haul Gizmo into her arms, then gather with the others around the fallen body of Agent Loulou.

Beneath the bridge, James had heard the awful noise of battle, and longed to go above ground to see what was happening for himself. Rags had forbidden it, however. After listening for some time, Gizmo told Rags he could no longer stay away from the fight and – apologetically – left Rags to guard James while he hurried off to do what he could to help.

James tried to listen in to the voices, but everything was chaotic and he could make no sense of the confused cries. He stared unfocussed, at the underside of the bridge, while he tried to separate one call from another.

As he was doing so, he realised that the faint light from the van had revealed something red wedged into the stones which, as he focussed on it more clearly, began to look very much like a wire.

Despite the terrible noise of events that were going on metres away, he could not help but think it odd. So much so, that he turned to Rags and pointed towards the wire.

"Rags, what's that?"

Rags followed James' gaze and his brow creased, if possible, even more deeply.

"That," he said, "is … really, really … bad news."

CHAPTER 29

MORE PROBLEMS

WHEN THE STRANGER witnessed the arrival of the van, he backed away into the darkness. It could only be Lifelink, though he had no idea how that was possible. He left Zin, the Doberman, to take charge and silently made his way in the dark across the bridge to its Southern end and a short way along the bank. The sound of fighting continued as he ducked down on the other side of the river. The night was loud with cries over the babbling water, but the Stranger still heard sub-verbally the sound of arguing, as it struggled up the bank towards him. Almost invisible in the gloom, two bedraggled weasels were clawing their way up the slope. They stopped short when they became aware of the human presence.

"Stranger?" A small, tinny voice. "We were just …" The voice trailed off but the other weasel demanded, shrilly:

"What are *you* doing over here, anyway?"

The Stranger smiled.

"Living to fight on - as you are? If you *are* leaving, however …" He let the sentence hang in the air for a moment. The weasels fidgeted. "Then, you could ensure a message gets to Titan for me. Find a hawk to carry it." The already-wet weasels shuddered. "Tell him Lifelink found us, but that the Stranger has … a backup plan – and that I'll see him soon."

He waved a hand at the small creatures, dismissing them, and they scurried on. The Stranger knew the weasels would find a way to deliver the message. They would be too afraid they might be found if they did not. Weasels, he thought scornfully, they had so little actual loyalty.

"Titan, old friend," he murmured into the night. "You will have to forgive me for this man-made solution. I know you didn't want it done this way."

He crept down towards the riverbank and felt around for something in the grass. After a moment he began to walk, head down, further away from the bridge for several hundred yards, checked the grass again, and climbed back up the bank. The Stranger then sat, cross legged, fixated on the dark space where he knew the road to be, waiting. At one point, he almost took action, when he saw a single headlight approaching from the South. His hand twitched in anticipation, but the sound was wrong too.

A motorbike swept over the bridge and the Stranger breathed harshly out and shook his head. Minutes later, all sounds of fighting had faded away. He heard Zed's furious shout, followed by the whining of the dogs, and anger flared inside him. But the Stranger held fast to his plan, and waited, his fists clenched, watching for more headlights.

Down near the river Evie, and the rest of the group, stared in despair at the fallen van. She had set Gizmo down on the grass and was now crouched near the prone body of her teacher, listening to the others. Agent Em whispered to Agent Zed, though they could all hear her perfectly.

"I have to get her somewhere. It doesn't look good. That's just too much blood, Zed." Loulou still had a pulse, Evie could feel it occasionally beneath her fur, but it was faint and she was unconscious. Her wounds were too many to count. Not that the Doberman had been left unscathed – he had hobbled away into the darkness, torn and battered. Zed's voice was as loud as Em's was soft, but he seemed to find it difficult to force words out nonetheless.

"Agent Loulou. You stood up well, to a much … to a – very strong opponent. We're, we're all, immensely proud of you. Eh … Lou?"

Evie thought Agent Zed sounded as lost as she felt, as he waited for a response. Loulou remained still and silent. Agent Em tried again.

"We need to get her home, Zed. She needs a blood transfusion, painkillers, stitches, at the very least. But here, in the middle of nowhere, with no transport …?" Agent Em's voice wavered and she stopped speaking.

Grandad! James sent his voice across the bank towards the lights.

James? Came the response, but his Grandad's voice came out shakily even inside James' mind.

Grandad, I'm still under the bridge. I'm with Rags. Are you OK?

It's Loulou, Grandad replied. *We need to get her some help, fast.*

James felt tears rising up but tried to not let them fall.

But … but Grandad – I saw a wire. While you were all fighting. And Rags says – he says it's a

bomb. Grandad, there's a bomb under the bridge!
Grandad's voice returned with its usual force:

What? James – you are both to get as far away as possible. I'll move the rest. Never mind about the coach. Go, now!

"What!" Agent Zed exploded, making Evie and the others jump up and scan the darkness, reaching for their weapons. "I'm a fool!" he said. "I thought they were done." Evie was staring at Agent Zed, totally unprepared for what he said next:

"I just spoke to James. The Misants have set a *bomb* under the bridge – Rags and James found it. I told them to get away." He turned towards Loulou, holding out his palms as if calling on heaven for assistance. "We can lift her – Ash, come over here."

Michiko drew close to Zed and placed a hand briefly on his arm.

"Agent … sir," she said. "The bomb can't be on a timer. You know what that means, don't you? Somewhere out there –" and here she scanned the darkness, which seemed to go on for ever, "is this Stranger, with his hand on a detonator. That means he is still waiting for the main prize. As soon as those headlights hit this bridge, that bomb is going off."

Em spoke, very quietly: "A few Lifelink operatives would be a nice addition for him I'm sure."

"Ash." Michiko's voice was now firm. She smoothed her hair down flat and tucked in her filthy shirt. "I want you to walk up the road and watch for the coach. The driver will have been briefed not to stop for anyone, but you have to make him anyway."

Ash turned and set off down the road without a word. Agent Zed took a deep breath, and nodded once, towards Michiko.

"Right, then. The rest of us need to move as far away as possible. I have no idea of the size of the blast. I need you all to help me with Loulou. Gizmo – can you walk?"

Evie swallowed the lump in her throat once again, as the little terrier with matted and bloody fur scrambled to his feet, saying:

"Don't you worry about me, Agent Zed."

The group began to move, very slowly, with their precious – but enormous – burden, along the road north of the bridge.

Under the bridge, James had relayed Grandad's message to Rags, but couldn't help asking a question of his own.

"Rags? If, like you say, the bomb isn't on a timer and he's waiting for the coach to set it off – well, doesn't that mean it's safe until then?"

Rags took a moment before replying.

"If you mean do we have time to get away, yes – don't you worry – we have at least until the coach turns up I should say. That is what you meant, right?"

"Well, no," James said. "Actually, I was wondering if we had time to disarm the bomb. They do on TV, don't they? Only we came here to save the coach and if we just leave – well, there's still a bomb." Despite saying all this so matter-of-factly, James could feel every second ticking against his skin. He imagined the night being lit by headlights again at any minute, and then blown wide open. He just couldn't stop thinking about the people on the coach as well.

"Ah," said Rags. "Your Grandad wants me to get you out of here."

"I know." James had been studying the wire. "But you can't reach it on your own can you? Grandma and Grandad are trying to save Loulou's life. I was listening in. I don't know how they'll get away very far. And I don't know how big the bomb is. Don't you see?"

Rags sighed.

"I do. I expect your Grandad does too and that's why he said to get away. You're too young for this boy."

"I'm too young to lose my grandparents and friends in an explosion too," James said, "and I want you to help me. If you can? Please, Rags?"

Rags stood up, fists clenched at his sides.

"OK, lad. Well, we're just wasting time now then. I need you to climb onto my shoulders and I'll stand up. If you can reach the roof, feel around the wire for a loose brick. There's something tucked away in there. If you can get a hold of it, fetch it down – *ever* so gently, a'right? And, if we hear an engine, we run, and hope."

With a great deal of difficulty, James hauled himself up onto Rags' back and held on tight as he was raised slowly upwards to touch the brickwork above him.

"Can you. Keep. Still – maybe?" James said, through gritted teeth, as he balanced with difficulty on Rags' shoulders. Rags himself was struggling to balance on the muddy path under the bridge. James blinked grit from his eyes and peered once more at the device wedged into a hole in the brickwork above him. He used Rags' screwdriver to pry the wire out all the way up the brickwork then attempted to do the same with the box-like bundle that clearly contained the explosives. It had been wedged into a hole where some bricks had been removed, and dust and dirt showered down as he worked.

"One. More. *Go*." Suddenly the bundle slipped downwards and rested in his hands. He screwed his eyes shut and waited, not breathing, feeling the blood rush inside his ears. Rags' voice sounded distant:

"What's going on up there?"

James opened his eyelids a millimetre or two, allowed himself a small breath, and whispered as loudly as he dared.

"You, er, you can let me down now, please … I'm, holding the bomb."

Rags did not answer. He swallowed, licking dust from his lips, and backed closer to the wall. He tried to bend at the knees, wobbled and stood back up. Just then a shadow blocked the entrance to the bridge and James felt two strong arms grab hold of him.

"OK Rags, you can let go now. I've got him." Grandad hefted James down onto solid ground, and kept hold of him for a few seconds, before carefully letting go.

"What, exactly," he said, glaring at the package in James' hands, "do you two think you are doing?"

"It's my fault," James said quickly. His Grandad lifted an eyebrow at Rags, who looked away. "No, it is – I wouldn't go."

"It's OK James," Grandad said, resting his hand on James' shoulder and giving it a small squeeze. "I understand. So – what now?" He turned to Rags with a frown.

"Well, now I have a bomb, that needs disarming quick." Rags lowered himself to the floor, shoved his grimy sweatband backwards on his head, and extracted a few small items from a pocket in the leather toolbelt he wore. As he spoke, he was studying the brick-sized parcel James had passed to him, which now rested on his legs. "How about you guys go up on top and watch for that coach? In case we have to run for it." James and his Grandad hesitated. "Don't worry. I'm not planning on being a hero. You'll be no safer up there than here. Unless either of you has been hiding the fact that you're an explosives expert? And I need to concentrate …."

James and Grandad both shook their heads and turned away, to head back towards to the road, leaving Rags to investigate the package.

"Can't you just cut the wire, hrrr?" said Mr T, regretting it immediately, as his voice from the darkness made Rags jump. Even so, Rags held the explosives perfectly still in front of him. He glanced around.

"Agent T?" he said.

"And Agent Artemis," Mr T added. "At your service."

"So," Artemis hissed. "Can't you?"

"That's good thinking, agent," Rags responded quietly, still concentrating on exploring the package with delicate fingers. "But there might be a second wire in the red casing of that tether that'll set the bomb off regardless, if it's cut. Short of an x-ray, I've no way of knowing. So instead … I need to work out how this little lot … fixes together…" He had continued to work with his fingers whilst talking and had gently removed a small amount of covering. He shook his head as droplets of sweat ran down his forehead, escaping the grimy headband. The light from the van was dimming now.

"Ah, I might be able to help there, hrrr," Mr T said. "I can see heat."

"What?" Rags did not seem to be paying proper attention, so Mr T repeated himself.

"I can see heat. With my left eye. Agent Em had to replace it years ago. It's like your night vision goggles. So, as I was saying, hrrr … the wires, you know – they generate heat – it's called 'resistive energy.' I learned a bit about it, after I got the eye." Mr T did not want to brag, but he didn't think Rags was really understanding him. "So – did you just want to know how many wires there are inside the cable, then? I mean … if it helps."

"Dear Lord, yes," Rags said. "How many?"

"Two."

"Oh." Rags' voice was flat with disappointment. "OK then," he sighed, a shaky sound. "Back to … disarming … a … bomb."

Rags' hand was hovering over the hole he had opened in the package. He held a small pair of pliers. Inside, Mr T could glimpse four wires: two from the cable and two attached to some form of battery. They were all green.

"Agents … that coach is gonna to be here any second. And, if it isn't, that Stranger bloke is going to blow up this bridge anyway, in the hope of getting back at us. So – if I can't solve this in the next five minutes, I'm gonna have to cut one of these wires. You might want to go and tell the other agents up on the bridge – the boy …." He smiled but Mr T thought he seemed sad, nonetheless. Just as he said that, though, James himself appeared and said:

"Oh! Hi everyone. Rags, I didn't want to speak sub-verbally – in case I startled you … ?"

Mr T quite forgot to say 'hello' to James, as he was distracted by Rags – who was shaking his head and staring wide-eyed at them all.

In the darkness, the Stranger became aware of two pinpricks of light gradually becoming larger. It had to be the coach at last. Then he spotted the much smaller light, like a faraway match in the darkness moving very slowly. Through gritted teeth he muttered the word "torch" as he understood what he was seeing. One of the Lifelinkers was flagging down the coach. It would never even get to the bridge. They must have discovered the bomb.

His last remaining hope was that the coach wouldn't stop. They were bound to have briefed the driver and he would be suspicious of being flagged down like this. If the coach did stop, he would blow the bridge anyway. It would be the only thing left to him. He knew there were Lifelink agents down there somewhere and they needed to suffer for their role in all this. That much he could still do. The pair of lights and the tiny match inched towards one another. As they did, the headlights began to slow down and the Stranger gripped the detonator tighter, watching.

Out of nowhere, the night was ripped apart - by an almighty booming, crashing sound, that made the air itself tremble. Water spray fell like a shower of cold rain, spattering even as far as the Stranger. He dropped the detonator and reflexively shielded his head with his arms, yelling pointlessly into the terrific noise surrounding him: "*No!*"

The distant lights of the bus stood still. The match went out.

Evie was desperately searching the haze in the darkness, where the bridge had been, as the air shook all around her with echoes of the explosion. She could make out nothing through the rain, the mud and debris. Her ears still rang with the blast and with her own scream. Agent Em had leapt up from where she had been crouched examining Loulou's injuries. The other agents' shocked cries fell unheard into the confusion. She could just see their mouths moving in terrified faces. Agent Em was standing completely still; her face had gone slack, and Evie realised that they had no idea where several of their group were - including Zed and James. Without considering what she was doing, Evie screamed into the night once again but inside her head: *James!*

Evie could hear only blood thumping through her ears, more a rhythm than a sound. Peering into the darkness, she waited, feeling more alone than she had in all the years she had lived with her secret voices. The only words echoing inside her head now, were her own, and the world felt more vast and empty than she had imagined was possible. Evie closed her eyes against the darkness and confusion and pictured them in turn: Zed, Artemis, Mr T, Rags – and James. She had been so angry with him, but he was just a child. He was twelve years old and he should have been allowed to reach sixteen, and twenty-six, and the rest of his life. He was an annoying, big-headed, spoiled child, but he deserved more than this. They all did. Evie imagined picking over the rubble and destruction and she was bitterly afraid of what they might find. Why did it have to be like this? Why couldn't everything just be OK again?

Why couldn't you just answer me, James! she screamed into the blackness.

Evie…? Evie was as stunned to hear the faint voice in her mind, as she had been by the blast itself. She gathered her thoughts in a hurry and shouted, silently, once more:

James? Are you OK? Evie had no idea what she was doing, but he seemed to hear her anyway.

Yes - I have Grandad and Rags, and Mr T and Artemis – we're all here!

It took Evie a few seconds to take that in, because it didn't make any sense at all – how were they all safe? Then she tried shouting out loud to get Agent Em's attention - before realising she couldn't be heard. Everyone was still deafened. So she went over and grabbed Em's arm, shouting straight into her face instead.

"Em, they're alive – James spoke to me. Zed and James and everyone – they're OK."

Em continued to gaze at Evie for long moments, seemingly completely unable to reply. Tears were streaming down her dirt-spattered face, but they fell either side of a smile that Evie watched spread like sunlight in the darkness.

Zed staggered to his feet. He had been knocked to his knees by shock more than anything. As he turned away from the cloud of spray and sludge, he caught sight of a silhouette stumbling across the skyline.

"Stranger," Zed growled, his mouth dry and the air dirty. He took a few steps after the figure, but stumbled a little and stood still, watching it vanish into the darkness. He waited to regain his breath and, as he did so, another figure appeared running towards him from the road, the dim light of a torch running out of battery bobbing up and down beside it.

"Zed! What happened? Is anyone hurt?" Ash was sprinting towards him, his face scrunched in concern.

"The coach?" was all Zed managed in return.

"I never even spoke to the driver, Zed. He turned it right around as soon as we heard the explosion. I don't know where he's headed now, but it's not this way."

Zed began to laugh and, when he did, he laughed so hard that tears began rolling down his cheeks, making tracks in the muck that had gathered there.

"He turned it around, Ash. If only we'd known - all we had to do was set off - a *bomb!"* Zed took several gulps of air. "We didn't give away any secrets after all." Zed was shaking his head now. "Ash. We have to get out of here. Before the police come." He started to head towards the riverbank, but stopped, realising Ash was still waiting, to add: "They're all OK. We have my grandson to thank, you know." Zed shook his head, chuckling, gazing at the wreckage of the bridge, lying across the broken river in a heap of rubble. "That boy, Ash, that boy."

CHAPTER 30

MUDDY WATER

JAMES, WATCHING THE others pick their way over the rubble towards the road, thought they looked like zombies in a video game. Nothing felt real. His team were all walking stiffly, with injury or exhaustion, their clothes ruined by blood and dirt, the landscape around the bridge destroyed. He himself was soaked to the skin, shivering inside Grandad's massive jacket, which he wrapped tightly around himself like a blanket.

The lights from the van had finally died in the explosion. There was moonlight, but they were relying on the torches. As the group clustered together it became apparent that both Rags and Gizmo – who was resting in Rags' arms – were also soaking wet and shivering violently. Michiko shrugged off her jacket and began wrapping it around the pair, struggling to close the zip at the bottom to keep it in place. Evie took off her woollen cap and jammed it onto Rags dripping head, with the words:

"What on Earth happened, Rags?"

"Oh, nothing m-much." Rags grinned at James from a grimy, mud-splattered face. "It was all p-part of the plan." James saw Evie glance around at the wreckage.

"All?" she said.

"Yes!" Despite his clear discomfort, Rags seemed cheerful. He lowered himself gently onto a boulder that had lodged itself near the roadside. "We have James, and these two, to thank." He nodded over at Artemis and Mr T, who had appeared silently and were now curled up side by side, in the centre of the group. They were both trying, and failing, to straighten out their matted fur.

"It was muthing," Mr T commented through his grooming.

"Speak f'y'self," said Artemis. Followed by *"Oww,"* as she adjusted her position to sit up a little. James listened, smiling shyly, as Rags settled into his story.

"Agent Zed told me to get this young man out of there, but *he*," here Rags gestured at James, "had other ideas. I know we should have gone, but the lad wanted to try to disable the bomb and, honestly, I wasn't sure we'd get far enough away anyway – so I'm afraid, I said Yes." Rags held up his hands to say 'sorry'. Grandma glared at Rags, her mouth set in a grim line, but Grandad put his hand on her arm and she said nothing. "Between us, we got the bomb down, but it was tethered by the wire that led back to the detonator. I'm guessing that was all he had. On the TV they use wireless stuff – just a phone call and off it goes. Lucky for us, he didn't –"

Evie spoke up:

"No signal. You can't use your phone up here, Rags."

"Oh, yeah. Right." Rags sucked his teeth as if he were thinking something but carried on. "So anyway. I wondered about cutting the tether - the lead cable, like - but Mr T here was able to tell me that was a bad idea, because he could see there was a trigger wire – meaning, if I cut the cable, the bomb would go off anyway." Mr T purred quietly for a second despite his bedraggled state. "So I thought I'd disarm it – you know, open it up and cut the red wire or whatever – but once I got inside it wasn't that obvious and I was running out of time. I was going to tell everyone to run for it, to be honest, maybe try and cover the bomb myself, before the blast." He shrugged as the others started to interrupt and carried on so they couldn't: "Then James here turned up with an idea. D'you want to tell 'em, kid?"

James was suddenly feeling incredibly tired. He hadn't noticed until now, sitting down at last on another displaced rock. He coughed to find his voice, and spoke up.

"Well, it was just science class." James paused and wondered if that could truly have been just two days before. It seemed like years. "We did water. I remembered it has a 'much greater density than air' and that when 'an object is propelled through it there is a decrease in energy.' I got both of those right you see, in the test. We were all worried that we wouldn't get far enough away. Then I thought, well the bomb wasn't in the bridge any more and it could go off at any time – but also, really, any*where* – that the, er – tether – could reach, anyway. And so I figured if it went in the water, the shock waves wouldn't go so far as they would in the air. You see? So I went to tell Rags." James stopped. His voice was getting a bit croaky now. For some reason, he noticed Grandma seemed to have stopped being angry and was starting to smile. Rags took up the tale again.

"So anyway, James said we should pop it in the river – genius! Then I had an idea. We figured this Stranger bloke was going to set the bomb off regardless – coach or no coach – so we suddenly thought why not use that to *our* advantage and beat him to it, right? Cos now I knew for sure - if we cut the wire, it would set it off. We didn't want to leave an unguarded bomb even under water, in case the coach got through, and we didn't want to be around when it went off – but of course we didn't have to be!"

Rags chuckled and looked around at the chaos, then smiled at James.

"I had about fifteen feet of wire to play with, so I waded out into the water and James passed me the bomb. The current was pretty strong in the middle, so James got in too. I held onto him, and he placed the bomb as deep as the wire would let him, so neither of us got swept away. Easy really. Then we climbed back out – and legged it. Meantime, *these* guys followed the wire up the hill. We figured the detonator would be at a safe distance so, if they were somewhere near that, they'd be safe too. Just not so near they got spotted."

"Hah," Mr T said. "He never even saw us, hrrr. Sitting on top of the slope watching the other way – it was kitten's play."

Rags continued.

"I told Artemis here to sever the wire as soon as they saw headlights in the distance. Near enough to hear and see the blast, far enough away not to see us. Brilliant." James saw Rags' face become serious then. "We could have done with another minute though - piece of debris hit Gizmo on his way to find us and he's already pretty messed up from that fight."

Rags shuddered and James saw him wrap the little terrier a bit tighter in the jacket. Gizmo studied Rags' face.

"You know I'll be OK, right? Not so good now, I grant you, but *I'm* not the one we need to worry about."

Rags suddenly looked around the group.

"I forgot! How is she?"

Grandma, who was still sitting beside Loulou, in a small circle of torchlight answered Rags.

"She's alive. She comes to, every now and then, but she's not really with it and she's out again now. James, how's Grandad doing?"

"He says he found Ash and they're nearly at the bike." James replied after a moment. Grandma looked over at Artemis, then looked closer.

"What's happened to you, agent?" she asked.

"Oh, nothing. All in the line of duty," Artemis said.

"Line of duty, maybe, but *not* nothing." This was Rags again. "She's been electrocuted Agent Em!

Using those fancy new claws you gave her to cut the wire for me. We assumed the voltage wouldn't be fatal, but other than that we didn't have a clue how the charge would affect one of your … smaller operatives … Brave stuff, agent."

"Right," said Michiko. "We can't rest any longer. We have to get this Bernese Mountain dog over that river to the bike. Rags, you help Gizmo. Mr T, Artemis, you might need a hand from James here if you're hurt? Agent Evie, you, myself and Agent Em, we will lift Agent Loulou together, on my mark…"

Mr T interrupted her.

"You might want to hang fire a moment there, agents."

James turned to follow Mr T's gaze. Where the bridge had collapsed, there was a pile of rubble making a dam across the river. While they had grouped together around Loulou, two figures had come stumbling out of the murky darkness. Mr T had heard them approaching over the sound of the water and conversation.

"Ah," said Michiko. "That'll help."

Grandad and Agent Ash joined the group, heading straight for Loulou and lifting her pretty easily between them. Stumbling and wobbly, the ragged crew made their way across the flooded bricks and debris, getting even wetter and muddier as they did so. James lifted both cats into his arms, much to Artemis' disgust, but he decided not to give her the choice. The river was pouring slowly and sludgily over the wreckage, pooling against one side and trickling away on the other. Over the bridge, they stood together everyone getting their breath back.

"I can't see any alternative but to rest the agent across the bike." Grandad said. "I think I can get her back to Ops West if I go slowly. I don't know what the journey will do to her though – and of course I can't take you as well Em." He paused. "Do you think … you could ride the bike, Em - with her?" Before Grandma could answer, Evie called out:

"Lights! Look!"

"The police?" Michiko said. "Could the coach driver have called them already?"

No-one replied. James and the others all watched as a vehicle sped towards them along the invisible road, headlights winding through the night. Grandad waved the group away, urgently, towards the darkest areas of grass. Then James watched as he laid the Harley on its side, with great care, some little way from the blast site. He sat himself down at the roadside, resting his head in his hands, and waited. James understood the act, as he lay still in the dark, watching what happened next.

The engine became louder and the lights closer, until the vehicle drew to a halt a few yards away and a figure jumped down onto the road.

"Hello?" it called. "I'm here from Lifelink?"

Grandad jumped up, a grin splitting his filthy face.

"Who on Earth are you?" he called.

James and the others began to come forward, out of hiding. As they did so, a smaller shape appeared from behind the driver's door and flapped some largish wings, before landing on the roof.

"Agents Rhys and Teegan, Ops Wales. So … who dropped a bomb on this place, then?"

CHAPTER 31

REGROUP

J AMES HAD BEEN lulled to sleep, on the long drive back to Ops South, by the Land Rover's rumbling engine. Before he drifted off, however, Grandad had received a call and been able to update them on the rest of the group.

He told them how Michiko had stayed at the scene, with Rags and the fallen post office van, to deal with the police. She had explained how 'she and Rags had had a lucky escape, not actually being on the bridge itself at the time the bomb exploded'. The police, seeming not to want to discuss the event in more detail, had not detained either of them or asked any questions and had even given them a ride back to the cottage – where a freshly showered Ash (dropped off by Rhys) had greeted them and pretended great surprise. Rags was apparently trying to organise a tow truck, so he and Gizmo would be back at Ops South as soon as he could get the van going again.

James woke up as the Land Rover came to a stop and the engine was switched off. Through the dusty Land Rover window, he saw the well-known front door of 45 Cromwell Street. His brain felt like it was made of cotton wool and he blinked several times before recalling what had happened in the night.

Someone was speaking to him. He rubbed his eyelids with the heels of his hands, lifting his head off the back of the seat.

"Time to get out, friend. Is that your Mum?"

Through the window James saw Mum running down the garden path.

"Yeah." He grinned at Rhys. "Thanks for the lift. Say goodbye to Teegan for me?" Teegan was asleep in a purpose-made owl box in the back. James wrestled with the door handle and the door swung open with a creak. He saw Grandad, who had followed them all the way on the bike. James scrambled down and was promptly swamped by Mum, squeezing him so hard that he gasped for breath. Then she held him away a bit and said:

"Oh, good grief! Look at the *state* of you! The *filth*!" Despite that, James found himself once more locked in an iron grip as Mum held him tightly a second time.

"Am fide, Bub, hon'st." James said. He was speaking into the woolly material of Mum's cardigan and wasn't sure she heard him. Just then, however, he heard Grandma's voice.

"Helen? I'm sorry love, but I'll need your help. She must weigh a hundred pounds!"

James and Mum turned around to see Evie and Grandad struggling to heave the shaggy mountain of Agent Loulou from the back of the Land Rover.

"Oh no!" Mum's voice was higher than usual and she released James, running over to assist them. They all manhandled Loulou through the house and into Ops, the two cats limping in beside them, before Rhys bade everyone goodbye and headed straight off back to Wales.

James followed the others into Ops, but was shooed back out again by Grandma. He had assumed he would help, like he usually did. Back in familiar surroundings, James started to realise how much had happened in such a short time.

"Grandma?" he asked, his voice wobbling a bit. "Loulou will be OK now, won't she?"

Grandma and Mum made eye contact with each other for some seconds, just as if they were communicating sub-verbally even though he knew they weren't.

"Grandma?"

"We will do the best we can for her, James. We will always do that," Grandma said in reply, "but you have to let us do it now. Go and find your Grandad, please, James."

James wandered out of the room, feeling unwanted. In his head he was determinedly picturing Loulou well and back to her old self, nosing around the living room. In the living room instead, however, he found Evie – sitting on the sofa, slumped, her head resting on her upturned palms, her hands covering her face.

"Evie?" he whispered. She didn't move. "Evie? Are you OK?"

Evie raised her chin a fraction and let her hands fall beside her legs. She stared straight at him, shook her head a little and frowned. James couldn't think of a response and slowly backed away towards the kitchen. In there he found the more reassuring figure of his Grandad, pouring boiling water from the kettle into mugs. The two cats were seated, side by side, on kitchen chairs pulled back from the table. James flopped down onto another.

"Ah, James," Grandad said, as if it were just any day at all. "Juice?"

"Er, yes, please. Thank you," James said, but added: "Grandad, I'm really worried. About Loulou."

"We all are," was all Grandad offered him, heading to the fridge. "Agents? Do you want anything?"

We just have to wait now James. Mr T had his eyes closed, but was clearly very awake. *Let your Grandma and your Mum work. Artemis needs her rest and so does Evie. We just need to get through today. Whatever happens, we'll face it together.*

James reached out and stroked the dishevelled ginger fur, then drew a finger over Artemis's head for good measure. James realised how exhausted she must be, as she didn't even complain.

It was hours later before Mum and Grandma reappeared from Ops. By this time, they were all sitting in the living room. The TV was on, though no-one had been watching it, all quiet with their own thoughts. Everyone was now showered and wearing clean clothes. The cats were groomed, and they looked much more like their normal selves, having slept most of the day. James noticed the humans' faces, however, were all pale with shadows under their eyes, giving away their deep tiredness. Grandad clicked off the TV and they all turned to face Grandma.

"There's nothing to do, but wait." Grandma spoke softly and her eyes were very red. "I'm going to change now." She left the room and James heard her footsteps trudge gradually up the stairs.

"I'm going to make a start on supper," said Mum, addressing the group. "Then maybe we can chat? Em has told me everything." She headed for the kitchen, but turned around again before leaving them. "I cannot believe that man was Jake," she said. Her voice was dull. James thought she sounded as tired as they all were. "We were better off before, not knowing anything," she added.

"I know," Grandad said. "But now we do."

Mum sighed and left the room. There was a moment's silence, broken by Artemis who was, once more, seated on the windowsill.

"So," she mewed "What's happening now? This Stranger – what are we going to do about him?"

Grandad answered her.

"I spoke to Agent Singh several hours ago. It's agreed Lifelink has to find out who he is - what he wants. And, of course, that would be good for everyone here, to know for sure, too."

"So, how do we do it, hrrr?" Mr T purred. "How do we find this Stranger and confront him?"

"Singh has a plan." Grandad said. "He has a link to a hawk who used to be a Misant. Titan almost killed her by all accounts and she swapped sides pretty smartly. He's thinking of using her to pass on a message. He wants to pretend to set up a meeting with a Lifelink defector. It would be an agent, of course, undercover …" Grandad stopped.

"We'll have a while – to find someone – then," Artemis said. "I mean, it won't be a quick thing to set up, will it?"

"No," said Mr T. "It takes time to earn people's trust."

Grandad carried on.

"They'll just need to decide who to send. *I* would have chosen Agent Loulou, of course, but …"

"I'll do it!" Evie said suddenly, making James jump. Evie had been silent for so long, he had forgotten about her. "I'll be the defector. It's got to be me, Artemis or Mr T hasn't it? We know the most. We've been involved. And it can't be either of you." She carried on, speaking quickly. "I mean, apart from you having business to attend to here, they'd *never* believe it if you defected. Rags and Gizmo are civilians. James is a child. As for Artemis, she has history, and Mr T …" Evie fell silent. Mr T and Artemis, from chair and windowsill, opened their eyes a little wider and looked steadily at Evie. James felt a little surge of anger that Evie had dismissed him, but at the same time he felt he couldn't really argue with her point.

"To *some* extent, you are quite right." Grandad nodded. James noticed the corner of his mouth twitch as he looked over at the two cats. "You are, however, still our least experienced – and probationary – agent. Not that last night won't have taught you a thing or two, and not that you didn't acquit yourself well – you *really* did. I just think we might need someone a little more … wily, somehow. Er, how are you feeling now, by the way?"

Grandad was looking at Artemis, who stretched out a paw, extending her claws, before answering.

"I'd say I was in perfect working order, agent. Raring to go ... Would there be hawks, do you think?" She flexed her prosthetic leg one more time. Grandad smiled:

"Possibly, but – if the time comes – if you see one that can't fly, leave her alone! She's on our side now."

James wondered if there was any chance at all he could, somehow, get to meet with this hawk.

Later that evening Mr T heard the doorbell sound and followed Agent Zed to open it, wondering if Rags and Gizmo had returned. Instead, it was a well-groomed middle-aged gentleman with warm brown eyes and an impressive nose.

"Singh!" Zed called out, loudly. "Why didn't you say?"

Agent Singh came inside, then stood in the hallway waiting for Agent Zed to usher him further. "Zed – and *Mr T!*" He said. "It was a spur of the moment thing." Agent Singh held out his palms and shrugged. "And, I thought it might be rather fun to surprise you? I was seeing the local MP, you know. One of our *less* exciting operations, eh? To do with the RSPCA rounding up strays ... Anyway, anyway – I realised I was but a stone's throw away – so."

"You are more than welcome, Singh, more than. Come through."

Mr T knew Agents Zed and Singh considered themselves old friends.

"I also wanted," Singh continued, "to meet this rather amazing grandson of yours. I must say, the Doughty family is becoming renowned throughout Lifelink – er, in a *good* way that is!" The three had entered the living room now and greetings were made all round. Agent Em had rejoined them and seemed much better than she had earlier. Helen was introduced, as was James. "Well, Mrs Doughty," Agent Singh began.

"Helen, please."

"Helen. You must be immensely proud of your boy here, eh? And I gather you yourself are part of the team now, all onboard, as it were? That's jolly good to hear, I must say. Good to see you again Artemis and – *Evie,* some news!"

Evie jerked her gaze upwards, startled, and Mr T could almost sense her nervousness at being spoken to directly."

"Yes … er, sir?" she said.

"Hah! *Good* news Agent Evie - you hear that? *Agent!* Not Probationary Agent any more. I should say you've done more than enough to earn your spurs – eh, Zed?"

Agent Zed made a sound of agreement. Mr T nudged Evie's leg.

"Oh, yes – thank you. Thank you very much. Sir." Evie said, reminded of her manners. Mr T pushed his head against her hand reassuringly. He felt very proud of Evie and wished Loulou could have been there to hear what Agent Singh had said. He suspected Evie wished it too.

The family had been about to eat supper. Grandma added bread rolls, cheese and sausages to the salad, quiche and potatoes Mum had prepared and James helped her arrange it all into a buffet. Grandad opened a bottle of wine and offered a glass to Agent Singh, while Mum sorted out drinks for everyone else. They each took a plate and helped themselves to food in the kitchen, taking it through to the living room to eat. Grandad had moved a couple of dining chairs and everyone was soon comfortable. Artemis and Mr T rapidly polished off their plates of cold chicken.

Over supper, Agent Singh chatted away as if he were quite at home. James listened to the conversation, feeling warm, full and safe. He could feel a bubble of happiness growing inside him, but it popped whenever he thought of the missing member of their group. Agent Singh was talking again.

"So, I spoke to that driver, Rags, and his friend Gizmo. They did sterling work, sterling, couldn't praise them highly enough. Civilians, eh! Broke all the rules in the book of course, but really, very good. I offered them both the position of trainee agent." James glanced up from his plate, excited. "They declined," Agent Singh continued. "Said this way they managed to get quite enough of the action, but could still turn around and say no!"

Agent Singh broke into loud laughter, echoed by chuckles from everyone else. Everybody, including James, helped to clear away after supper. Grandma made coffee and they all sat back down again. The room was quieter now, people talking more slowly and quietly. James heard Artemis speaking, her high voice cutting through the hum of people chatting.

"We were thinking perhaps Evie and myself could take on the undercover work, now she's a proper agent. I know they've met me, but I can talk around that. Say I had cold feet – I'm sure I could come up with something. We know it's months away, there's a lot of groundwork to be done first, but that just gives us time to work on our back story."

Mr T joined in.

"Yes ... I believe the phrase is 'elephant in the room', hrrr? The thing no-one is saying, but we all want to know?" This last bit was for James' benefit as James had asked silently: *What?*

Mr T explained further.

"This Stranger, this Misant, the right-hand man. We all need to know who he is. If there is the slightest possibility he is linked to the disappearance of James' Dad, then we need to know it. I don't think it changes anything, mind, either way. He still needs to be stopped. But we all have a lot of questions he might be able to answer, hrrr."

The room fell silent. James suddenly realised Mum was searching people's faces, knowing she was missing out on something important.

"Mum," James said. "Mr T says we need to know if the Stranger is Dad."

"Succinctly put, young man," said Agent Singh. "Helen, my dear, I am sure the agent *we* all knew could never do such things." Mum smiled at Agent Singh, her eyes shining, and blinked several times. "Agents," he was now speaking to Grandma and Grandad, who were sitting side by side on a sofa. "I really do feel for you all. This is an unprecedented situation. One you could never have imagined."

 "No-one could," said a deep voice from the doorway.

Everyone started in surprise, looking around – and James felt happiness bubble all the way up into his chest – as Loulou came limping into the room. Evie and Grandma both shot over to her side, Evie's cheeks suddenly shiny with tears. James felt his face muscles stretched to bursting as he mirrored the huge smiles on all the faces in the room. Even Artemis stood up.

"Oh, I *say*!" Agent Singh exclaimed. Loulou stood patiently waiting for the fuss to die down.

"I couldn't help but overhear," Loulou said over the others' voices, "so I couldn't stay lying down in there."

Grandma seemed to struggle to force her face into a frown, then shooed her patient over to the hearth rug – where Loulou lowered herself uncomfortably, avoiding her various stitches. Evie plonked down next to her, despite her tears looking happy for the first time in days. The room still echoed with everybody's excitement. As they quietened down, Loulou raised her head, to address them in her old no-nonsense fashion – which made everyone smile despite the seriousness of her words.

"Whatever we find out *will* be bad. It can't be good news, of that much we can be certain. So, we need to formulate a plan, and get on with it. I assure you I, for one, will be right there on the front line. Both Artemis and I have scores to settle now and the Doughty family need Jake's good name cleared once and for all. So, the only question is – when do we start?"

Loulou paused and Agent Singh took the chance to address the group, taking a deep breath, and making sure he had their attention.

"You have all – every single one of you – been through rather a lot lately, even by Lifelink's standards. I can't tell you how grateful I am." He cleared his throat, and they waited. "Loulou is quite correct in her assertion that we need to begin planning. I would go as far as to say that, we are going to have to mount some sort of large scale defensive operation against this Stranger. Some sort of *attack* – yes, quite possibly." He looked steadily around the room, at everyone there in turn, including James. "So I want to be quite clear, here and now. *None* of you is required to volunteer. And I will be telling Agents Ash and Michiko the same thing." He had held out his arms, in a gesture that included them all. "This matter is too close to some of you, and *all* of you have been through the wringer, well and truly. You deserve to let the other regions take the strain for a while. Rest on your laurels and all that, while you recuperate."

Agent Singh gazed round at them all. James did the same, trying to guess the expressions on everyone's face. He thought most of them looked quite blank. He was aware of a hollow feeling opening up inside himself and blinked several times.

"Yes?" Agent Singh broke the silence.

Mr T was the one to finally speak up:

"That's *incredibly* generous of you, Agent Singh, giving us all a holiday like that. Just – a couple of things though, I think?" Singh nodded for Mr T to continue. As he did so, Artemis silently stood up and exercised her claws – out, in. James felt a broad smile, rising up from his chest to burst across his face, as Mr T purred: "May we all be allowed to decline the offer, hrrr? And - can we start right away with the plan?"

Printed in Great Britain
by Amazon

60633770R00206